SISTERS OF GRASS

Sisters of Grass

a novel by

THERESA KISHKAN

GOOSE LANE

Edited by Laurel Boone.
Cover image from Rubber Ball Productions.
Author photo by Charlaine Lacroix, 1999. Reproduced with permission.
Book design by Julie Scriver.
Printed in Canada by Transcontinental.
10 9 8 7 6 5 4 3 2 1

Canadian Cataloguing in Publication Data

Kishkan, Theresa, 1955-
Sisters of grass

ISBN 0-86492-288-4

I. Title.

PS8571.I75S58 2000   C813'.54   C00-900147-6
PR9199.3.K444S58 2000

Published with the financial support of the Canada Council for the Arts, the Government of Canada through the Book Publishing Industry Development Program, and the New Brunswick Department of Economic Development, Tourism and Culture.

Goose Lane Editions
469 King Street
Fredericton, New Brunswick
CANADA E3B 1E5

For John, Forrest, Brendan and Angelica Pass

The country of souls is underneath us, towards sunset.
— James Teit

Prologue

IN DARKNESS I HEAR the stories come down from the Douglas Plateau like a summer herd of cattle, ranging for grass as they move into the valley. Such beauty in their coming, rustling through rabbitbrush, bringing their ripe smell, their mouths working their way around clumps of bunchgrass. Each story has a separate mouth, yet together they tell something larger and deeper, as all the individual grasses — bluebunch wheat grass, sweetgrass, coyote's needle, the giant wild rye often found near gravesites — growing with the sedges and buckwheats, make up a pasture. I have walked in the high pastures, picking blue flax and brown-eyed Susans, scratching at the foxtail barley seeds hooked into my socks. On distant hills the cattle watched, mild-eyed at a distance, and from every draw, a story waited until the dark. I lie in the blue tent and listen.

I have come to find someone I know only through an impression, a packet of photographs found in a box of memorabilia. The box itself is a few slats of old wood, stencilled with Smith, Spences Bridge, Grimes Golden, lined with a cardboard carton. Unsorted, unsung: letters bound with faded rose-coloured ribbon; a program from a concert; newspaper clippings; a copy of *Camera Work*, dated Autumn, 1906; a length of thin, hollow bone. But the photographs have a voice: quick vowels of sunlight articulating reeds in a body of water, the studied language of horses, long dissertations of pastures, and, huddled together like the generations in a family portrait, decorated baskets on rough planks. On the envelopes, a name, Margaret Stuart, and an address, Cottonwood Ranch, Nicola Lake, British Columbia. And postmarks that tell their own narrative of travel: Seattle; Astoria, Oregon; Fargo, North Dakota; New York.

The letters have been so lovingly bound that I was reluctant to break their embrace, but I studied the photographs, carefully opened the magazine, read the newspaper review of a concert in an unlikely place nearly a century ago. The box has been donated to the small museum where I work and has sat in a dusty corner, waiting to be catalogued or for someone to arrive with an eye to filling in a branch on a family tree. A colleague said, Anna, this is a place you go to, isn't it, the Nicola Valley? Have you looked in this box yet? It might be interesting to see what's in it. So I put aside my regular work, columns of notation and surmises based on external evidence, and took up each item to look at in the clear light of day. A shiver ran down my spine, as though someone had walked over my grave. Yes, my family does visit the valley regularly, feeling a kind of belonging we never have words for, needing the dry air and birdsong. Yet our grandmothers and grandfathers never farmed there or recorded their dead in the parish books. Still, drawn by scent, by pollens, by the caress of wind filtered through the high branches of pine trees, we come to find what we can: the pattern of cattle trails in the aspen groves, a phrase of lark call, a lake named for a beloved daughter. And would it make a difference to have a history, even this briefest of histories, incomplete and fading, to link to plants and horses, settlements of graves in two locations — one alongside the plain board church in what was once a thriving townsite, the other on a gentle shoulder of field leading down to a marsh of blackbirds trilling in the rushes?

This could be any summer. We've driven here in sunlight and rain, though the rain never lasts long, only wetting the rocks to release their flinty smell and washing the sagebrush and mulleins lining the roadsides clean of their dust. On one stretch of the road, erratics sit impassive among the sage, and marmots whistle from their shoulders. How long ago did those erratics ride the glacier down to this slope? They sprout a few pale, dry lichens, crisp to the touch. Cattle rub against their warm sides, leaving tufts of coarse hair.

We have been to the Douglas Plateau in all seasons, driving up in summer to drink a thermos of coffee after dinner while the children turned cartwheels in the falling light, driving up in winter to see what the groves of cottonwoods looked like, bare of leaves, the ponds and small lakes brittle with ice. Once, in autumn, twenty, perhaps thirty, horses approached the truck, their eyes calm and curious. I took apples from a paper bag and walked to meet them, a girl again among horses. One, a bay mare with a star and white socks, came up to me, lowering her head so that I could rub between her ears and pull a few burrs from her forelock. She wouldn't touch the apples but blew softly through her nostrils as she sniffed my hair, my face. It was though we'd known each other all our lives and had just been reunited after a long absence. I've smelled her since in various winds, salt sweat and pungent grassy dung, and I've dreamed of her, dreamed that I vaulted onto her back the way I'd mounted my own horse years earlier, balancing with a handful of mane. I have a photograph of her, taken by my husband from the safety of the truck, and I've thought of approaching someone — but whom? — to ask about her. Do you know this horse, I imagine myself asking, can you tell me where I might find this horse? But then what? I can't think how the story might continue.

I lie in the blue tent and listen to the little brown bats, straining my ears to catch the pulse from their larynxes, seeing shadows of their wings on the walls. By day they roost between the bark and cambium layers of standing dead pines, coming out a dusk to hunt insects. When we walk, we see them flitting between trees. Once we found a dead one here and examined the odd wings, like fine leather, the fierce face reminding me of a wolverine.

Some nights I've stood out on the slope by the lake in moon-

11

light to see what I could see. The dark silhouettes of loons, moving lights coming down the Pennask Lake Road, disappearing as a truck rounds a hidden corner, visible again in the open, the moon passing across the sky like a soft lamp, and once a spade-footed toad on its way down to the lake to cool off. When the traffic is scanty and the campers few, I feel as though I'm seeing the valley in its innocence. Nothing but the animals following their nocturnal habits, climbing out of holes in the sand, swimming from the safety of reeds to bask in moonlight, taking wing in the dry air. Big moths fly toward the candle on my picnic table, and before I can call a warning in a language resembling moth, the delicate wings have sizzled to ash.

I hear the stories coming down from the high plateau, attended by coyotes and burrowing owls, the tiny swift shape of a bat. One might be her story, Margaret Stuart of Nicola Lake, a gathering of small details that might make up a life. Weathers, generations of insects to riddle the fenceposts, a swatch of muslin from a favourite gown. The grasses are beautiful in moonlight — pinegrass, timbergrass, brome grass, giant rye. *And now it seems to me the beautiful uncut hair of graves.*

Chapter One

I AM ARRANGING an exhibit for the small museum where I work. I've wanted for some time to look at a period in the history of a community through its textiles. Mostly this will show the history of the women, although I would be happy to be surprised. I put a notice in the local newspaper, asking people to bring in textiles that might be a part of the exhibit, and I have phoned those whom I know have collections of suitable objects. There have always been quilters, for instance, and I hoped to find generations of quilts showing common family themes. I know also of a few women who made samplers for grandchildren. One of them told me that her family had always done this and that she still had the sampler her grandmother had made for her as an infant. One elderly woman makes lace, something I remember my own grandmother doing, even when she was very old and blind. With fine cotton and a thin crochet hook, she made lengths of fragile webbing which fell from her hands to her lap and then to the floor.

I am thinking, too, that the exhibit must include objects from the various cultures that have called this place home. In the museum's collection, there are pieces of clothing made by the aboriginal people — skirts of cedar bark, diapers of fine inner bark, hats and capes, blankets of yellow cedar bark. And there is also a small jacket, a child's jacket, of indigo cotton, padded and quilted with tiny white stitches, that I'm sure must be Japanese

13

sashiko, although its card reads, "Donated by the Williams family, provenance unknown."

But pieces are slow to come in, and I've been looking into the box which I've come to think of as Margaret's box, the name on the letters evoking a girl, perhaps the girl in one of the photographs, standing in a field with one hand shading her eyes. She is not smiling but looking towards the camera, her shadow falling to one side of her like a faint sister. And little by little I am trying to piece together a life from the small scraps of ephemera.

William Stuart: Astoria, 1883 — Nicola Valley, 1887

What William remembered most about his boyhood in Astoria: boats and horses. His father had been a bar pilot on the Columbia River and made sure that his son learned to manage a boat and navigate the dangerous sandbars at the entrance to the river. Standing in the pilot house, he pointed out the way the ocean currents moved against the steady surge of the river, how the sandbars endlessly changed so that a man had to keep his eyes open, to be constantly alert to weather and seasons. To know which birds were swimming in the grey water and which were perched on submerged hummocks of sand. Together, father and son went over and over the compass and the elder Stuart's annotated charts, faded handwriting indicating rocks or testily questioning the fathoms. He was less than happy, however, when William secured summer employment with a school friend's uncle, Jim MacKay, helping on a gill net boat.

"Remember, William, that we are descendants of the Stuart kings!" This was his refrain whenever his son threatened, by word or deed, to shame the family. Yet the elder Stuart's beginnings had been humble enough. A descendant of Scottish royalty? Perhaps — a small pool of blue blood in a forgotten hollow, a crook of the elbow or deep in the ribcage, ignored by generations of red blood coursing by in the daily work of the living. But his own immediate family had been Highland crofters and had sent him to North America during the Clearances. He'd survived by his wits and natural intelligence, marrying a daughter of John Jacob Astor's paymaster and with her building a comfortable life on the rim of America.

The Astoria they knew was a bustling seaport, with the first post office west of the Rockies, the first customs house west of the Mississippi, and a bevy of stately houses clinging to the steep slopes, one of which was their house, with its hipped roof, its balconies and verandas, its three-storey tower that looked right out to the estuary. On a good day, watchers could spot eagles and harrier hawks, black-shouldered kites, blue herons returning to their rookeries, plovers and murrelets, pelicans, and deer making their careful way across the sand. In immaculate copperplate, William's mother kept a journal of her sightings. *June 12, 1882: Using the telescope, I watched an eagle swoop down over the water and pluck a merganser chick from the clutch following the mother as she swam in the shallows by the entrance to Youngs Bay. Too far away to hear anything, I could only imagine the distress of the adult as she tried to protect the other five chicks from such predation. Also seen: three herons, bufflehead, a magnificent osprey and two sea lions pulling themselves up onto a islet. I think they must have been feeding on the candlefish that are making their way by the thousands up the river.* Her son would come upon her at such times and watch her hand moving across the paper, followed by a script as lovely as the scribble of bird tracks in the sand. Leaning to read over her shoulder, he could smell lavender and violets and would remember her cutting tall stems of lavender in high summer to dry in airy baskets spread about the floor of the attic, stripping the dried flowers later to fill muslin bags to tuck into the linen. Her fingers would be fragrant with the oils for some days afterward.

But William convinced his father that he was old enough to

know his own mind, and the way he wanted to spend his summer was on Jim's boat. And anyway, from what he'd learned of the Stuart kings — Charles I, James who was sent to France, the Old Pretender, the Bonny Prince who'd come back to the island he'd heard about since his infancy in Rome ("A salvo of guns sounded from the Castle of St. Angelo") to claim his true crown — William felt they would approve of the decision he had made.

He didn't talk about the work much at home. How to explain the feeling as the tow-boats pulled the fleet out past the mouth of the river and then released them one by one to the wind and tide, how he'd row and steady the boat as the nets went down, the mesh shoaling into the grey water? He would imagine the curtain of net across the current, the fish entangling themselves silently in the barrier. He loved pulling them in, splitting the lines, cork to one side, lead to the other, while Jim removed each fish, hitting it once firmly on the head and then putting it to rest in a box he would cover with damp burlap. Every muscle in William's body ached as he held the boat steady in the waves, even after he was accustomed to the work, and for the first few weeks, the palms of his hands were raw with rope burns. Until they callused, he'd wince every time he gripped the ropes, the salt water stinging. Putting the wound to his mouth, he tasted salt and blood, a tang of seaweed, thinking how remarkably close to fish was this blending of elements.

It wasn't so much for the money that he stayed on the job, though when the price for sockeye went to three cents a pound and the run was good, he would come home with more money than he'd imagined possible. At night he and Jim slept in turns in the doghouse, fragments of dream interrupted by wind and the push of the tide against the keel. When Jim was sleeping, William would sit out watching the lantern bobbing on the far end of the net, lulled by water. He thought of the song his mother had crooned him to sleep with, always saying, "And this was your ancestor, my son. His blood runs in your American veins."

Speed, bonny boat, like a bird on the wing,
Onward, the sailors cry.
Carry the lad that's born to be king
Over the sea to Skye.

He'd imagined the child lying in the bottom of a small skiff ascending skyward, a look of astonishment on his face. At dawn, they'd pick up the net and find another drift where they could set it again, they'd make tea on the Primus and some sort of a meal. But it was for the run back to the cannery that he wanted this, when they'd raise the spritsail, sometimes even a second spritsail or a jib if they were running before the wind, and it was like flying low over the water, the sails flaring. Sometimes two or three of the gillnetters would go in together, racing in the wind like giant butterflies. William's heart was in his throat as he tacked and turned, gulls in their wake, the treacherous sandbars hidden in the white-capped water. Each safe return seemed a miracle. William had never known such freedom.

Passing Sand Island, they'd see the beach seiners taking out their nets in small flat-bottomed skiffs, then leading huge horses into the tide to pull the nets in. The horses waded belly-deep in icy water, received the lines, then turned, straining as they hauled the fish-laden nets to the shore. Jim MacKay told William that they'd take in thirty tons of salmon on a good day. The cries of the seiners, urging the horses to pull, pull ye lazy bastards, and the snorting of the teams, their sides sleek with water, their shoulders lathered in sweat. Passing near them, William could smell their sweat, cut with the iodine tang of the water, the cold odour of the salmon teeming in the nets. The horses were like unknown creatures, rich and strange, dressed with seaweed, more at home with gods than men, calm as mountains. After them, the Stuart horses seemed so sedate. A matched pair of Morgans to pull the carriage, a saddlehorse or two, they lived in a tidy stable behind the house, snorting primly from the small cinder paddock where they were turned out while the stalls were cleaned. A man cared for them, harnessed them when the carriage was required, and he was not too pleased to have a small boy — later, a young man — hanging about. The bridles were more like ladies' gloves than like the tack worn by the river horses, thin strips of fine leather, the brass polished to dull gold. The Stuart horses had delicate buckles at their throats, jointed snaffles between their jaws; the river horses wore their harnesses like armour, girdled in straps, mighty curb bits clanking in their mouths.

William liked to take his father's mare up to Coxcomb Hill, where he'd let her graze on the young grass while he followed the routes of the rivers with his eyes — the Lewis and Clark coming in from the southwest, Youngs River immediately south, the mist-covered Columbia surging from the east. His tutor once showed him reproductions of quattrocento paintings, and the rivers looked here and there to be painted by the same hands. They made him restless and homesick at the same time, the clear green of the surrounding trees, the contour of the rivers disappearing into fog. He wanted to venture up each to its end, and yet he was afraid of what he might discover hidden beyond that soft curtain. There were stories told in Astoria of men going into the wilderness and never coming out, their footprints vanishing into thin air. The woods teemed with stories of huge hairy creatures, half-human, watching from a ridge, valleys of trees too large to get the mind around. Jim MacKay had worked in the woods, and he told William about cutting down cedars near Mist, then inviting others to join him for a dance on the stumps. "I've seen four couples," he said, "aye, four couples waltzing on the dance floor created by a stump, while two fellas sawed away at fiddles and another lad played a mandolin alongside, balancing on the springboards." Below, in the town, William could hear saws whining at the mills, the commotion at the docks as crates of canned salmon were loaded onto waiting vessels. From this hill he'd once seen whales, a stately procession passing the estuary. The natives hunted them, he knew, using the bladders of seals as floats for their harpoons, and whaling ships came into port for provisions, their decks bloody, the piles of whale flesh stacked carefully to balance the load. But the day he saw the whales, they moved north, their progress unimpeded by anything more than curious seals.

Two summers of working with Jim MacKay convinced William that he ought to buy his own boat. He didn't tell his father but chose one himself, a twenty-six-and-a-half-foot Columbia River salmon boat. It was white with blue gunwales and beamy enough that he felt safe handling it himself. He bought it in February, 1883, and spent a few months down at the docks, scraping the bottom, tarring the inside planks, repairing the nets, patching a hole in the jib using stitches taught to him by his sister Elizabeth. He enjoyed being around the other fishermen, listening to them tell stories of good years and bad. Most of them fished for the cannery and used the cannery boats; they worked on these during the off-season for an hourly wage, labouring over them as carefully as if the boats were their own. William tried not to ask too many questions but watched and learned with his eyes and hands. Sometimes another fisherman would take William's hands in his own and draw the scraper over the curving wood of the hull, helping the young man to feel the pressure needed to pare off paint and barnacles, though barnacles were few here where the boats were moored in fresh water or lifted to the quays for the off-season. He'd smell the bitter edge of the pipe tobacco the Norwegians smoked, the unwashed sweaters of homespun wool, the thin, vinegary whiff of pickled salmon, pungent with mustard seeds.

That was a good season for him. The runs were enormous, the nets teemed with fish, and the canneries worked around the clock to keep up with the supply. Sometimes when he delivered the fish, he would look inside the cannery; he saw the native women expertly cleaning and slicing the salmon, the Chinese men making cans from tin plate, soldering them together, the steam swirling from the processing baths, the smell of fish and blood entering his nostrils in nauseating gusts. Everywhere the gulls wheeled and cried in the wind. A good season, yes, but when the sockeye finished that year, he decided to sell his boat and try something else.

Some enterprising men recognized the need for beef in the gold fields of Williams Creek and Antler, and a few decades earlier, they'd begun driving herds of cattle there from Oregon and Washington, taking them over to the Boundary country, across brigade trails, and up the wagon road running north from Yale. The uncles of William's friend Tom Alexander had participated in the drives, and their stories fuelled Tom's adventurous spirit. After a summer with his uncles, he had come back to Astoria with shining eyes, telling of huge ranges of grass, there for the asking. Some of the drovers had settled to raise cattle on the rich bunchgrass, and although there were no longer the big drives of the fifties and sixties, it was possible to find work on a smaller, more specialized trip north, one bringing solid breeding stock, mostly bulls, to established ranchers trying to improve the quality of their beef. A herd of Clydesdales was making the journey, too, for the ranchers wanted good teams to pull the haying equipment. William slipped away from his sleeping house one morning, leaving a note.

The trip north had been glorious, riding through the coulees and grasslands of eastern Washington territory, swimming the animals across rivers, up through the Boundary and over to the Thompson Valley. William remembered campfires under stars, the unearthly howling of coyotes, and an unsettling moment when one of the drovers found a rattlesnake curled up under his bedroll. He'd cut off the head without a moment's delay, and then expertly removed the skin for his hat band. Waking at night, William heard the Clydesdales snorting and shifting in the darkness, and he remembered the powerful shoulders of the horses pulling in the seine nets, water bedraggling their fetlocks.

When the group arrived at their destination, a ranch in the Hat Creek Valley, they'd all been paid, and then William travelled to Kamloops to gather his thoughts. He paid for a room in the

Cosmopolitan Hotel and got to know the owner, a man called Edwards, who told him it was a country ripe for young men. Ranches, paddlewheelers, contractors blasting away mountains for railways — there was work any place you cared to look. Edwards lent him a horse, one of the muscular wide-chested mounts favoured in this area, and William rode in every direction, trying to get a sense of place.

He'd never seen anything like it, this country of golden grass. He couldn't remember when he decided for certain that this was where he wanted to spend the rest of his life: he stayed one winter, then two, working for Bill Roper at Cherry Creek after a tip from Edwards, who knew all the ranchers. He lived in bunkhouse, learning from the other men, acquiring a saddle which he couldn't then remember living without, though it was certainly different from the saddles he'd learned to ride with in Astoria in what seemed like the life of another young man. He discovered that the winters were bitterly cold and the summers hot, nothing like the moderate seasons of his boyhood, tempered by the Pacific. People spoke of chinooks, warm winds that could come during the coldest months, they spoke of the spring flowers; even the spiny cactus would produce enormous deep yellow blooms, some tinged with apricot, some fading to soft red. In the fall of 1886, on a selling trip to Joseph Greaves at Douglas Lake, William had looked at the vista from the Douglas Plateau, the sky that billowed and rolled forever, dark with thunderheads, the oceans of rippling bunchgrass, and he asked a few questions about ranches.

It turned out the Cottonwood place was available. As a ranch it wasn't much yet, but the title included six thousand acres of grass, both deeded and commonage, and he wasn't afraid to work hard to build it up. He bought eighty head of two-year-old Shorthorn steers and moved them to his ranch, fencing one big meadow with the help of a young Indian man from nearby Spahomin to keep them in that winter. There was a cabin, nothing fancy, two windows with glass intact, a roof of split cedar shakes, only a few missing, and, once he'd cleaned out the stovepipe of mice straw, a useable stove which almost warmed the room he lived in. At night he'd hear mice in the other room, and he knew a packrat was nesting underneath the floor boards because of the sharp stink. As soon as he could, he would get a dog to deal with the packrat. He re-chinked the biggest gaps between the logs with clay and moss and built a log frame for his bedroll, but he did little else to the house. It was more important to get the cattle through the winter. At night he'd sit as close to the fire as he dared, the smell of his wet woollen stockings draped over the fender filling the small room, and he'd remember the old song, humming it to himself or singing a phrase here and there, never able to summon up the entire thing: *Onward, the sailors cry* or *though the waves leap, soft shall he sleep* or *dead on Culloden's field.* He could see the Highlanders fighting bravely but then slain in their thousands on the bleak moors of Culloden and Glencoe, which he imagined looked a lot like his own home meadow in winter. Some nights he didn't make it to his bedroll at all but slumped in the wooden chair, dozing while his stockings steamed. The ghost of his bonny ancestor stole from the field, dressed as a maidservant, secreted away to Skye, and returning finally to France, then Italy, no longer the gallant youth who had captured the hearts of the Scottish chieftains. The part his father had not cared to tell him, the tutor had revealed: Charlie ended his days a drunk and a cuckold and couldn't have done much for Scotland even if the Highlanders wanted him.

That winter was one of the coldest on record. William had been able to purchase a little hay, a few tons, and he'd scythed as much grass as he could, drying it quickly, then dragging it with a rope behind his horse to a central location, but his eighty head mostly had to feed themselves on what they could find. Unlike horses, who could paw away snow from a covered field and get at the wintering grass underneath, cattle were at the mercy of the elements. William had counted on them surviving on their stored fat and what fodder he could get to them. Another winter they might have been fine, but from mid-January on, blizzards brought snow to cover the grass and other forage, and in the spring of 1887, Cottonwood's winter pasture was dotted with carcasses; less than half his herd had made it through. William called the field Culloden after that and thanked heaven he hadn't been counting on cows to drop healthy calves after such a fierce winter.

When a letter came from Astoria, the first since he left though he'd written home many times — to tell them he had arrived, where he picked up his mail, about the ranch, how he hoped they were well and weren't bitter about his leaving — he knew what it would say before he opened it. He'd dreamed of his father's death a week earlier and had woken to find his bedroll soaked with tears. So the envelope edged with a thin black line came as no surprise. What he didn't expect to find out was that a large amount of money had been included in his father's estate for him. The money could be wired to him as soon as he provided the name of a bank. Such a loss and unexpected gain filled William with turmoil. He supposed this was his father's way to demonstrate forgiveness and approval: to have remembered the defector in his will. Yet how welcome a letter would have been in William's first lonely months. He went to Kamloops and arranged to have the money sent to the Bank of British Columbia there. It would be useful, no denying. He'd pay off what he owed on the ranch and buy some more cattle, maybe even invest in one of the Hereford bulls just coming into the country, thanks to Greaves of Douglas Lake, and a good string of horses. He'd need haymaking equipment, too, if he was going to increase his herd and keep more horses. And he ought to make some improvements to his cabin, which looked more like a home now that he had received a parcel from Astoria containing a mariner's compass quilt made for him by his mother and sister and a sampler cross-stitched by Elizabeth, soft flowers and a verse from the Old Testament: *Whose house I have made the wilderness, and*

23

the barren land his dwelling. The range of the mountains is his pasture, and he searcheth after every green thing.

The day William first saw Jenny was in the autumn of 1887. He'd gone to Father Lemieux's house by the church just a mile or two from the Cottonwood Ranch to pick up some books. Not a Catholic, he had been gifted with a classical education nonetheless (for this was how the Jesuit put it to him) and had taken to dropping in to drink port on occasion and take home volumes selected for his edification by the good Father. Thomas Aquinas, Duns Scotus, the confessions of St. Augustine, and even texts by earlier intelligent pagans, Pliny and Cicero — these had been taken to the windy cabin and read with great interest and a fair amount of skepticism on long evenings. And sometimes there was delight of recognition, as when Pliny described the mares of the Portuguese. William pondered over the Latin, *Constat in Lusitania circa Olisiponem oppidum et Tagum amnem equas favonio flante obversas animalem concipere spiritum, idque partum fieri et gigni pernicissimum ita,* wondering if the mares would gather themselves into a circle and hold their tails up to facilitate copulation with the wind. It was not difficult to picture them lifting their tails, he'd seen it so many times. But to the wind? Well, perhaps. After all, he had seen the gusts of ripe grass seed moving in currents of warm air, seen the golden pollen of cottonwoods falling from the sky. And maybe Pliny offered as complete an explanation as any for the occurrence of certain swift horses when the bloodlines did not lead you to expect such speed. And he laughed aloud in his cabin as he read the section of the Natural History concerning superstitions. *Rumpi eqos, qui vestigia luporum sub equite sequantur* — horses would burst if they were ridden in the footsteps of wolves, as near as he could tell. He hadn't yet heard of wolves in this territory, although there were coyotes, cousins no doubt, and this theory might explain the way horses spooked when they heard coyotes nearby at night.

He found pondering these things exhilarating. He had no time to read in spring and summer, and only now that he had his herd down in Culloden for the cold months ahead did he find himself with a few hours to drop in on the priest. They chuckled over Pliny but agreed that he got so much right about weather and the behaviour of bees that one could forgive his lapses. It was Aquinas the priest loved. With winter coming, William would take advantage of his leisure to exercise his rusty powers of logic in debate with that austere mind. He kept a rough journal in which he noted ideas of particular interest or phrases that rang in the wind.

We next consider how one creature moves another. This consideration will be threefold: (1) How the angels move, who are purely spiritual creatures; (2) how bodies move; (3) how man moves, who is composed of a spiritual and a corporeal nature.

He would have liked to have asked Saint Thomas about cattle, which he, William, believed had something of the angels in their being. Or the huge fish he caught in the Thompson River once, its body muscular and shimmering with the colour of the sky. Looking into its eyes, he knew God. He wondered what Father Lemieux would have to say about that, or any of the saints, for that matter. Or what they would say about horses carrying the offspring of the west wind in their wombs, air turned to muscle and bone. Surely there was enough superstition in their own theology that they could hardly censure Pliny and his mercurial horses.

"Ah, William, come in. I'll have Jenny bring us some refreshment. Go in and sit by the fire."

The priest waved William into the cosy room at the front of the house and went off, his boots clattering on the board floor of the hall. Jenny? William wondered who Father Lemieux was talking about. His housekeeper, Mrs. Garcia's cousin, was called something, he forgot what — "the good woman" or "the woman who does for me" — but not Jenny. The priest returned, rubbed his hands in front of the fire, and then went to the shelves for a book he was hoping William would enjoy. A few minutes later, there was a soft knock at the door and a young woman entered with a tray of glasses and something warm wrapped in a tea towel. She was the loveliest woman William had ever seen. Indian, obviously, with her lustrous black hair pulled back in a knot and a dress of indigo stuff. Her features were fine and regular, and when she looked at him, shyly, she smiled with such radiance, her teeth even and milky, her cheekbones tawny and high. Leaving the men, she closed the door and went quietly back to the kitchen.

"Jenny is on loan from LeJeune," said Father Lemieux. "He's gone off to help with a church at Kamloops and to see to that newspaper he's become so involved with, and my housekeeper had to return home because of illness in the family. Jenny is a very able girl. LeJeune convinced her to work for him when he was building the church at Douglas Lake last year. One of the Jacksons. A good family, the mother one of the basket makers. Do you know them?"

William realized that one of her brothers, it must have been, had helped him with some fencing when he'd bought more cattle and needed corrals at the home site. August Jackson. William had found him companionable, easy to sit with around the fire at night, watching for shooting stars and listening to loons. The rest of the visit with Father Lemieux passed in pleasant confusion. William could think only of the woman in the kitchen at the back of the house, her supple brown hands as she arranged the glasses and other things on the low table, her smile. He couldn't speak of Aquinas or original sin or the merits of the port in his glass. When he left, carrying two books which would remain in his saddlebag for days and would be returned unread, he saw her face at the window, smiling at him in lamplight. *How the angels move.* He came back twice, once to ask her to attend an afternoon concert at Nicola Lake, and once more to fix a time for him to collect her so that they could be married by the Justice of the Peace, John Clapperton, at the courthouse in Nicola Lake. The priest had not been entirely happy with William "absconding" with his housekeeper, and he had not been pleased at all that Jenny was marrying outside the church. But he had come to visit them in the cabin at Cottonwood and had been reassured by the sampler, which showed evidence of biblical knowledge and suggested that the house would not be entirely godless; he gave them a Bible with gilded pages as a wedding gift. He had also left a bottle of his excellent port and told William he'd be by from time to time to hear Jenny's prayers and to drink his share.

Wanting to take a break from the textiles, I suggest a brief camping trip to the Nicola Valley. I have a report to read, preparatory to my exhibition, and will take some time to clarify the details of Mylar, adhesives, insurance against humidity and insect damage. Away from the objects, I can make a plan for their display. And I am hoping to figure out the geography of Margaret's box, the placement of trails and the locations of photographs.

When I wake the second morning after a deep sleep, I take a minute to remember where I am. Tent, blur of mosquito netting, Clark's nutcracker scolding in a tree just at the back of us. I have dreamed of a girl, waiting on horseback. It might have been myself half a lifetime ago, the same dark hair and straight back. Someone is humming outside, and the sun is already up; I feel heat through the nylon wall. I go down to the outhouse to pee and find moths all over the inside of the cubicle — noctuids, geometers, pyralids and tiger moths, wings spread for balance and camouflage, stippled with colour. I am accustomed to thinking of moths as the enemy, and I have seen the damage caused to fine woollens and silks by the larvae of brown house moths and common clothes moths. But the wings of these are like samite or the couched gold grounds on pieces I have seen in ecclesiastic collections. I forget where I am, lingering in an unseemly fashion among the toilets as I examine each moth, their eyespots, their antennae fringed with sense organs. A few in a heap into a corner of the cubicle look for all the world like dead leaves or the crumpled, foxed pages of an old book. Not wanting to disturb them, I resist the urge to poke at the little pile with a twist of toilet paper to see if they're alive.

Nicola Lake is lovely in the clear morning, ruffled a little by a light breeze, faint voices calling from the shore. I take back a kettle of water to make coffee and find our blue enamel pot covered with a fine yellow dust. Anywhere else, our stuff would be damp, condensation glazing the walls of the tent, the sides of the cooler, even our sleeping bags, but here we wake to pollen, falling from the pines like golden rain. I pick a small bouquet for the table, fleabane, asters, a sprig of southernwood. When the children come back from walking the dog, we eat pancakes with maple syrup, watched by a chipmunk on the nearest tree.

On a horse, dark hair, her back straight, her eyes shy.

Once, in this very campsite, I looked idly to the rocks behind us to see my image reflected in the eyes of a coyote. How long it had been there I had no way of knowing, but my children had been playing among the rocks earlier, and I wondered if it was attracted to their scent. It didn't stay after I looked into its eyes but slunk away up the slope, its tail low, looking back from a respectable distance to make sure I was watching.

Hum of bees in the tall grass, quarrel of crows, ache of the distant hills dappled with sunlight. Each morning could begin this way, each evening end with the loons. To have grown up in this air, taking in the dust of this earth with each breath, dust of dried grass, animal skin, the bodies of collapsing stars. I have dreamed of a girl. Pollen falls into my coffee as I walk among the trees, wildflowers brushing my legs. A startled ground squirrel skitters away.

Chapter Two

IN A HANDKERCHIEF edged with fraying lace, the smell of lavender. A few brittle seeds caught in the threads. I rub them between my fingers and am taken back to my own grandmother's house in Halifax, where hedges of the grey-leaved plants lined paths and where bundles of their dry flowers kept the rigid piles of ironed sheets fresh. Gifts sent from that coast arrived with sachets tucked into pyjama pockets or wrapped in an apron constructed of scraps of polished cotton and lengths of crocheted lace, the bittersweet odour rising from the box as it was opened. And this box, too, has its incense, a prelude to the rituals of discovery and accompaniment.

The air of the valley's history is rich with the smoke of artemesias burned to clean and protect, clouds of tobacco smoke bringing the souls back from the dead. And the smell of evergreens laid about to protect against witchcraft, illness, the tips rubbed on the bodies of girls to keep away evil. The rising of dust as graves are swept with the branches of wild roses. When we make our campfire, I burn a branch of sage for my own safe passage through this world of ghosts, my hands rich with the oil of lavender, Margaret's little bag of earth.

Margaret, Nicola Valley, 1904

She was riding in the direction of her favourite place, Minnie Lake, though she knew she wouldn't get that far today. There were tasks Mother wanted help with, and the younger children were still weak from the bout of influenza that had laid them low one by one; Margaret was the only one strong enough to beat carpets and begin to mend the winter quilts before they were put away until fall.

But today there was a fresh wind, and Mother told her to saddle up Daisy and go for a ride.

"I can manage for a few hours," she said. "Tom is sleeping and the girls are playing. You go. A ride will make you fresh. Bring back some sunflowers if you can find them in bloom."

Daisy had been easy to catch, though a few of the other saddle horses rolled their eyes and trotted away as Margaret approached with a handful of oats and a bridle. She tied her horse to the fence while she changed into trousers in the barn. This was the compromise she'd reached with her father: she could ride in trousers but had to change in the room where they kept the harnesses. How he could have imagined it possible to ride in a skirt, even a divided one, was beyond her, and why her riding clothes had to change just when she'd turned fifteen puzzled her, too. That was when he'd decided that she must cultivate a more ladylike appearance, helped by his visiting mother and sister from Oregon. They showed her how to roll up her hair, after brushing it a hundred times, showed her how to starch her petticoats with sugar until they were stiff as boards. Her mother only watched, saying nothing. Her own soft dresses moved as she moved and did not rustle.

When Grandmother Stuart and Aunt Elizabeth had arrived in Forksdale for that visit a year ago, Margaret's mother had not wanted to ride down in the buggy to pick them up. She would prepare food, she'd suggested, make sure everything was ready, the beds well aired. The ladies would disembark from the train at Spences Bridge, spend a night there at Mr. Clemes's hotel, then come by stage to Forksdale, stopping along the way for tea at Coutlee. But Margaret's father had insisted she come. At the livery stable, her mother had kept in the background as embraces and kisses were exchanged between her father and these two handsome women in their fine hats. Introductions were made, her father leading her mother forward by the hand. Grandmother Stuart and Aunt Elizabeth had known Father had married a native woman, of course; he'd told them in letters. And in 1890, in exchange for beef, he'd had Dr. Sutton photograph Jenny, holding the infant Margaret, at the settlement at Nicola Lake, the portrait carefully framed and packed up to send to Astoria for Christmas. Grandmother Stuart and Aunt Elizabeth wrote long letters to the family several times a year and sent parcels for the children. But this was the first meeting, and the first time William had seen his kin since 1883.

Watching Jenny Stuart greet her mother-in-law, Margaret thought how beautiful she was. She wore her glossy hair in a braid, and when she brushed it out before bed it looked like dark water in starlight. She'd grown up first on the wild grasslands near Douglas Lake and then, after 1878, in a cabin on the Spahomin Reserve. She had been educated by Father LeJeune, one of the missionary priests, after showing a quick intelligence and curiosity, working as his housekeeper until Margaret's father had married her and taken her home to Cottonwood Ranch, near the north end of Nicola Lake. In those days, the ranch house had been the two-room log cabin which the cowhands now slept in, there was no garden, barely a barn. Jenny had worked hard with William, helping to string fence, digging over a large area to grow potatoes and turnips to store for winter, planting slips of roses and crabapple seedlings given to her by other ranch wives. In turn, she helped them with cooking during the haying season until the Cottonwood operation grew large enough to demand her every minute. She had become an excellent ranch wife, a gentle mother, fond of music. When William played his violin, she closed her eyes and leaned into the melody, sometimes humming, never singing. And beautiful, yes, but not like the women in Margaret's father's family, with their elaborate dresses and high voices. Jenny was quiet by nature, not shy, exactly, but a woman who chose her words carefully and never learned the art of small talk. Grandmother Stuart took Jenny's hands in her own and told her she was looking forward to seeing the ranch and getting to know her daughter-in-law over the next two months. Jenny smiled and looked to Aunt Elizabeth, who, after exclaiming over the mountains they had seen from the train, the pitch-dark tunnels drilled through the rock, the beauty of the river below them, wondered about tea.

"The cup of tea at Coutlee was very pleasant," she said, "but its effects have not lasted long!"

"You must be so thirsty," said Jenny. "I've brought some refreshment, it's in the buggy. Shall we put your baggage in, and then I can get you some lemonade?"

William and Tom carried the smaller cases to the buggy, and then Mr. Armstrong, of the livery stable, sent out a boy to help lift the bigger trunks. The horses moved restlessly, their harnesses jingling a little. Jenny reached under the seat for a basket and offered everyone a drink. The children all took a tin cup of lemonade, but the ladies chose to wait. Margaret heard Aunt Elizabeth comment to Grandmother Stuart about the unseemliness of eating and drinking right there on the street. "Ah well, my dear, we are hardly in Astoria now," was Grandmother's tart reply.

Remembering that first meeting, Margaret felt a pang for her mother. The two women from Astoria never really got to know her, preferring to spend time with William and the children, reminiscing, telling the children funny stories about their father's boyhood, or else working on a sampler they left with the family: vines and flowers around a collection of birds in a potted tree above the adage, *He doeth much who doeth a thing well.* The younger three children loved their presents of books, a model ship in a wavy glass bottle for Tom, and lengths of pretty calico, smelling of dried lavender, to make up into dresses for Jane and Mary. Margaret's gift was a dresser set, a silver-backed brush, comb and hand mirror, and a bottle of French cologne. She was a little afraid of using such beautiful things, but Aunt Elizabeth soon had her hair unbraided and was brushing it out in long strokes.

"Such lovely hair, Margaret. I'll show you the way all the young ladies in Astoria are dressing theirs now. And here, a little dab of this scent behind your ears and in the hollow of your neck. There! What do you think?"

"I've never smelled anything like it. What is it made of?"

Aunt Elizabeth told her about the fields of flowers — jasmine, rose, lavender, orange blossom — cultivated in the south of France; she'd seen them on a tour of Europe taken with Grandmother Stuart two years ago. "We stayed in Grasse, my dear, and in the evening you could smell the flowers as the night air released their oils. This cologne comes from there. Sublime!"

Margaret had smelled roses, of course, the ramblers growing around the veranda of their house and the wild pink ones close to Nicola Lake, but the other flowers were unknown to her. France she knew from the atlas at school. Privately she thought she preferred the sage of the hills all around her, particularly the way it smelled in the morning after a rain, tangy and warm. And the scent of hay as it was raked up behind the team. Timothy, clover, lucerne and rye so sweet and pure it made her feel faint.

Astoria, 1906. *My dear, I must confess to you that I had never seen hair as pretty as yours. I remember brushing it out with the silver brush and how it flowed down your back. I look at the photograph your father sent after that visit. How young you were! And I try to imagine you older but see only your braids, your narrow wrists. I still hope to take you to France to see those fields of flowers. We could stay for a time at Cap Antibes, a little fishing village where painters sometimes spend the winters and paint the Mediterranean. At least you must visit us here in Astoria. It is a very rainy town but such flowers as a result! Someone could take you out on the river in a canoe, where you would be travelling the same currents as the man for whom your own great river is named. Such things are endlessly possible.*

One day, her father offered to take the ladies riding. Grandmother Stuart declined, but Aunt Elizabeth was pleased until she realized they had no sidesaddle, just the usual stock saddles with long stirrups and high horns to hold ropes. She'd learned to ride at her boarding school as a girl and had definite ideas about proper style. She finally allowed herself to be coaxed, in her long skirt and fine buttoned boots, up onto one of the gentle geldings.

"That's the sister I remember," William announced, as she arranged her skirts around her with some difficulty. He showed her how to hold the reins in one hand and press them to the horse's neck to direct him. She laughed and waved her straw hat in the air.

"Do I look like a Wild West Show poster girl? It's a pity you haven't given me six-shooters as well. This saddle feels remarkably like a bath chair. I do believe I could ride all day in this kind of comfort."

"Oh, we often ride that long, and longer," replied William. "After six or eight hours, it doesn't feel like a bath chair, I can tell you."

Margaret came out of the house in her riding trousers, an old pair of her father's that Jenny had helped her to shorten and alter. She wore the soft buckskin jacket that her mother's mother had made for her, a design of stylized birds woven into the fringe with sage bark. Putting her face to her sleeve, she could just catch the faint aroma of burning sage used to smoke-tan the skin. Aunt Elizabeth was shocked.

"William, you can't let her go about in that ridiculous outfit. Mother would be horrified."

Obviously Elizabeth was accustomed to speaking her mind, and she expected her listeners to pay attention. Margaret, embarrassed, saddled Daisy as quickly as she could. She waited for her father to explain that she often rode with him for long hours, looking for stock or checking for kills, even riding as an equal hand on the cattle drives to Kamloops. After all, didn't he tell her often that she was his best cowhand, as good on a horse as any of the men? She could not work in a skirt. And how could Aunt Elizabeth call her clothing ridiculous? Grandmother Jackson's jacket was her pride and joy. She loved how the buckskin smelled, loved the design and the way the jacket felt like part of her own skin. But her father only mumbled a little about their isolation and the convenience of trousers and the fact that she was still a child. Margaret waited for him to defend Grandmother's sewing skills, her honour, in fact, as the most skilled woman in Spahomin with tanned skins and design. He began to speak of Grandmother Jackson's method for curing skins, but Aunt Elizabeth would have none of it.

"Really, William, you *must* insist on standards, even at this distance from civilization. The girl is very nearly a young woman, do you notice nothing? She will never be marriageable if you allow her to run loose like a ruffian, you must realize that. It's not as though decorum is unheard of in this country. The Smith girls at Spences Bridge, for example, we met them riding sidesaddle, in skirts. I'm certain their mother would never allow them to race about the countryside in old skins, astride a horse in such a provocative way. They are lovely girls and will marry well, I should think."

William Stuart was silent, looking first at his sister, then at his daughter. His face hardened as it did when he was angry, and his eyes were like ice. Then: "Margaret, we'll discuss this later. Now, please, if you will, open the gate so we can be off."

Margaret soon forgot her aunt's outburst. Who could stay angry or embarrassed for long under an arching blue sky in the cleansing wind? Up through the bunchgrass hills behind the ranch buildings to a small marsh, along the highest ridge so Aunt Elizabeth could get a sense of space, stopping in a grove of ponderosa pines to eat their bread and cheese and drink from a flask of cold spring water. Margaret pointed out a nuthatch creeping down one of the pines, and they could hear the tinkling song of a horned lark above them. Aunt Elizabeth rode well, catching on to the western style of neck-reining and holding her seat at the gallop. Her cheeks were flushed with sun or excitement, Margaret couldn't tell which.

At a high point in the calving pasture, William Stuart pointed out a golden eagle drifting down from its eyrie on Hamilton Mountain. He told his sister how unpopular they were in this country because ranchers blamed them for taking young stock, particularly lambs.

"But I've watched those birds all the time I've lived here, Lizzie, twenty-four years now, and I've never seen them trouble live calves or sheep. And I've seen plenty of eagles hunting rabbits and marmots, and fishing of course, which I really think they prefer. But some of the men shoot the eagles whenever they can, and it's a shame."

"William, remember Father telling us about golden eagles in Scotland? There was a bounty on them when he was a boy, and he earned pocket money shooting them for the laird. Now, would that have been because of the sheep?"

"Oh, likely. I've seen eagles feeding off dead lambs, yes, but there are lots of ways for a lamb to die besides under their talons."

They returned by a different route, the spring pastures, and William described something of his system for the cattle — how long they spent on each area of the range, how they were rounded up and moved, what range was best in which season. He loved the ranch, and it made him happy, Margaret could tell, to show it to his sister. She paid attention to what he told her and asked a few questions, teasing him about his accent, which she said was pure cowboy. Her own patrician voice betrayed her years at boarding school in Portland and at finishing school in Boston.

There was no more talk of the trousers, but later Margaret heard Aunt Elizabeth speaking to Jenny about the unseemliness of a young woman wearing trousers in a country full of rough men, only a few of whom were suitable for marriage. Jenny kept her eyes down and said nothing. This was not something she would decide; her husband knew about such things and would no doubt speak to Margaret later. Jenny had a difficult time keeping straight the social strictures to which she was required to adhere, however subtle or illogical. Clothing, for instance. The priests had worn the same black trousers, jackets, stiff white dog collars for everything but Mass. On the Reserve, the older people still wore moccasins of soft cured deerskin, decorated with porcupine quills and tiny glass beads when they could get them. They were perfect footwear for this country — setting traps, gathering berries and roots, even fishing, for they'd dry fast in the wind. But comments would be made when the elders went to town, behind hands to be sure but meant to be heard, and thus the younger people wanted the heavy boots that they imagined would carry them to acceptance. Jenny thought how regal her own mother had been in her tanned deerskin leggings and quilled shirt, and how small she seemed, in recent years, in her ill-fitting high-necked dress and cotton bandana. Such clothing seemed inappropriate as she sat coiling cedar roots for the baskets she made in the old way, piles of bark and fibre alongside for imbrication. And now this fuss over Margaret's trousers, as though the girl needed to think about marriage at her age. William would know what to do, she was certain.

But William decided to forbid the trousers in order to placate his sister, and it wasn't until some time after the two Stuart women had returned to Astoria that Margaret was able to persuade him that she could ride in comfort as long as she changed in the barn and took care not to be seen by anyone other than the cowhands. He had always allowed her a good measure of freedom and relied on her as a steady helper and companion around the ranch, trusting her judgement on important matters. But the trouser incident made him uncomfortable, as though he now realized that his daughter's mixed blood might one day put her at a disadvantage.

On the one hand, he'd come to this country partly to escape his own family. The Stuarts were among the elite of Astoria, with their elegant mansion and Chinese servants. A code of behaviour accompanied their position in the high house with its view of the river and the Pacific, unwritten but perfectly clear nonetheless. William's attempts to find his own way had met with bewilderment, then anger. His family hadn't understood his love for fishing, but at least he'd joined the Astoria gill-netting fleet, near enough to home that they could see him with the telescope as he came in from the sea. But fishing hadn't been enough, and when Tom Alexander had told him of the cattle drives north into British Columbia, William's nerves had stabbed him with excitement. He'd left early one morning for the Willamette Valley, not trying to explain in the note he'd left for his family, only asking them to keep him in their hearts.

On the other hand, he'd married Jenny, herself of mixed Thompson and Okanagan blood. Her father was from the Douglas Lake Reserve of Spahomin and her mother from the village of Shulus on the other side of Forksdale, towards Spences Bridge. Although Jenny had been living at the priest's house when William met her, she was closely bound to her family, and she still saw them as often as her busy life allowed. Her younger sister came to help out at the ranch during haying, and one of her brothers regularly brought venison and smoked fish, sometimes a string of ruffled grouse hanging by their feet, or a pheasant. They were fine people, William thought, and he hired many of their friends for ranch work. They knew the country, each grove of aspen with its story, every season with its texture and spirit. Once they'd invited him to participate in a sweat bath when he'd gone over to the Reserve to see who was available for a few days of branding. Jenny's brother explained that they generally went through a sweat bath before a hunting trip, but they were doing it now simply because they felt like it. William remembered heat, the smell of juniper and sage, the stones being brought in, huddled and hot in special blankets, the hissing of water as it met hot stones. There had been cycles of prayers for healing, for strength, offerings of tobacco strewn on the stones. He'd felt as if he was dying, the way the hot air seared his lungs, and he'd closed his eyes, trying to regulate his breathing, hearing his heart pound in his ears. Or was it the heart of the man who squatted next to him, the man who'd reached out and clasped one of William's hands in his own, saying something in the Thompson language that soothed William and gave him strength. His skin had tingled from the scrubbing with rough fir branches and the cold water, taken from the creek nearby, that one of the men had ladled over his naked body. Riding home, he'd watched the stars come closer and closer until he knew he could touch them if he'd only reach up. Everything shimmered, and he saw himself ride out beyond the road, enter the night, disappear into the velvet darkness like a red fox gone to earth. He heard an owl and the music of loons.

And today there was wind with the green smell of cotton-woods on it as Margaret galloped Daisy up to the place where she'd seen a pair of coyotes playing in the golden grass, where the whole valley spread out below her, and hawks hung on the warm thermals looking for field mice. She found spring sunflowers, the first yellow blooms of the year. Her grandmother had told her they always said a prayer before digging the roots to cook in the steaming pit or else snipping the new flower buds to enjoy as a spring tonic, and Margaret wondered if she should say something before cutting the stems with her bowie knife.

She closed her eyes and hoped a prayer would come to her. When such beauty opened itself to the world, springing from earth only recently frozen and bleak, there ought to be words to match the radiance. Not able to think of anything, she cut a brilliant bouquet and tied it to the horn of her saddle with a long strand of grass.

Wrapped in a piece of faded tissue, a worn jacket of deerskin, thin and soft, plant fibres woven into the fringing. Holding it to my face, I smell the earthy aroma of animal hide, of smoke and sweat, the skin like the inside of my arm. I am caught for a moment in a fragile web of emotions which keep me still and quiet.

A girl, riding the long slope of pasture, shimmering in the sunlight. *By what way is the light parted, which scattereth the east wind upon the earth?* And with what message does she come across the decades, yellow balsamroot, which some call sunflowers, hanging from her saddle?

Each item in the box of her life can be noted and commented on, and yet what distance between a jacket and its wearer, a little bag of earth and its connection to the human landscape, what distinction between photographs and memory, the way a place is remembered in all its colours and scents, the feel of its dust settling into the lungs. What a basket has known of camas roots and wild onions and the weight of longing in the fibres of the handles.

Chapter Three

THE FIRST SUMMER I came with my family to Nicola Lake, I had the feeling I was passing through a curtain into the past, that the present was only a moment imposed upon a history of such compelling presence that it shimmered and shone, oblivious to current events. *By what way is the light parted?* The houses in the townsite of Nicola, the ancient lilacs in the graveyard with seedpods withered and dry, the rain fences of cracked grey logs — all were rich with what had passed into memory. Standing on the roadside where we stopped to take photographs of the lake in sunlight against a backdrop of suede hills, I'd feel the ground rumble with the movement of cattle and horses and wait, vainly, for them to appear. There were never cattle in the valley in summer. They were high on the plateau, out of sight, and the fields around the lake were planted with hay crops — alfalfa with its sweet blue blossoms, timothy — and golden oats. On the road to Kamloops, trucks made their steady way north, windows open to the air.

We were a family gathered together by ghosts. Not our own, but dry sounds heard among those lilacs, in the hasp on the gate to the graveyard. Some of the enclosures around the graves consisted of pickets and square-cut nails, dark orange with rust, rough on the thumb as one or another of us touched the surface. There was pain in the shape, the rough touch, pain in the rustling of leaves, yet it was necessary as breathing. To walk quietly under the lyrical pines and take in the details of their

41

needles against a blue sky, to imprint the particulars of a time and place into the fabric of our own lives and histories, was as urgent as anything we had known. I saw my children staring across the water, their thin shoulders rising and falling as they took in deep breaths of that pollen-laden air, saw them choose perfect cones to tuck into their knapsacks. A fallen nail held in the fist like an amulet, branding their skin with the iron of place. Seedpods found their way into empty jars, pockets, a few feathers of a magpie stuck into the brim of a hat.

And now, years after those first visits, I am here to find a version of a girl. A date, some photographs that show a way of seeing the world, a path leading to a some rocks on a slope of pasture. The report on conservation has not given me a vocabulary to use in this search. How to allow for access without over-handling, or remember the watchwords "no interference" in order not to lessen the value of objects as historic documents.

Margaret: Nicola Valley, April, 1905

Margaret was riding up beyond Culloden, one of the ranch dogs trotting along beside her. Her father had asked her to watch for coyote signs. The neighbouring rancher was setting out poison baits, and the wise coyotes were keeping clear of that range. That meant more on the Cottonwood and Lauder ranches to the west and Douglas Lake to the east. It was a windy day with a few thunderheads to the north; Margaret had her oilskin tied to the back of her saddle and one of her father's old hats on her head.

On a west-facing ridge she stopped, dismounting to stretch her legs and take advantage of the view. She could see Nicola Lake, grey and choppy, to the west. Lauder's Creek, swollen with spring runoff, raced towards the Nicola River immediately south of where she stood, and beyond the Douglas Lake road, hill after hill of new bunchgrass rolled endlessly, effortlessly towards the horizon. The dog flopped down on its belly and fell asleep so suddenly and deeply that its feet continued where they'd left off, trotting in air and twitching, little yips coming from its throat. If there was a coyote in the vicinity, Margaret couldn't see it, though a pair of falcons tossed in the wind, and she could make out a small herd of mule deer grazing over near Lauder's Creek. She decided to let the dog sleep for a bit, so she sat down near a group of boulders.

Margaret leaned her shoulders against the largest boulder and felt something poking into the small of her back. Something hard and sharp. Turning, she could see the thing protruding from the ground about three inches, not a stick or rock, but something white and calcified. She dug around it with her finger, loosened it, pulled it carefully out of the earth. It was a thin bone, about seven or eight inches long, and once she'd brushed off light surface dirt, she could see a design incised into the bone's surface, dirt in the incisions making the pattern obvious. A series of parallel lines along a third of the bone's length, a number of star-like shapes in the middle third, and at the other end, crosshatching. Taking a long rigid stalk of rye-grass from a clump growing nearby, Margaret prodded it into one end of the bone. Dirt trickled from the other end, and she worked all of it out easily. By now the dog, wide awake, was watching something that looked suspiciously like a coyote creeping towards the mule deer in the distance. One coyote couldn't bring down an adult deer, she knew that, but this one might be part of a family pack, and the deer probably had young in their midst. Back to work, she thought, putting the bone, carefully wrapped in a bandana, into her saddlebag, mounting Daisy and riding off to investigate the area where the coyote was coming from to see if she could find its lair.

"Where did you find this?" Jenny Stuart asked her daughter.

"On a ridge just above where Lauder's Creek joins the Nicola River. Do you know what it is?"

"Yes, I do. Among my mother's people, these were given to

young girls who were learning to be women. I didn't have that training because we'd begun to go to church and then I went to live with the priest, but my mother did. Was this on the ground or under something?"

Margaret told her how she'd found the piece of bone. Jenny asked if there'd been many boulders around, and Margaret told her about the ones she'd been sitting among.

"Well, Margaret, you might have been in a burial ground. They were never around the houses in the old days, not like now, when there's always a field for graves beside the church or by a home. I don't know too much about it myself, but if you want to know more, why don't you go to see your grandmother for a few days? She likes it when you visit. See if your father can spare you."

William had no objections, so Margaret packed her saddlebags with a few personal items as well as gifts for her grandmother — a jar of crabapple jelly, a loaf of Jenny's bread, drawings from the younger children, a rooted cutting of honeysuckle she wanted to plant by her front door — and left mid-morning the next day. It was about six miles to Grandmother Jackson's small house on Spahomin Reserve, and the day was perfect for riding, with high cloud, a breeze, everywhere the smell of green leaves and budding sage.

By the time Margaret rode into sight of Douglas Lake, she was hungry and hoped that Grandmother would have one of her stews on the back of her woodstove. Jenny's brothers, now with families of their own, kept their mother well supplied with rabbits, grouse, fresh or smoke-cured fish from their gill nets. She often had visitors, for she was the elder with the deepest knowledge of plants; people came for advice on sickness or wounds and would leave with a poultice or a handful of dried roots or a salve. Payment was made in food or firewood, but she never turned anyone away who couldn't give her something. And no one left without a meal of venison stew or a piece of wild duck tucked into a bannock. Teas and decoctions brewed in a large kettle, the cabin always fragrant with rose hips or wild ginger.

Grandmother Jackson was standing in the doorway when Margaret rode up. She held Daisy's head as the girl dismounted. "I was not expecting you, but I'm so glad to see you here. Hobble Daisy and come in. The day is fine, and we can go up later to pick some sunflowers."

Margaret's grandmother was tiny and quick-eyed, her face a map of lines. She spoke English slowly and carefully, measuring each word, saying exactly what she needed to say and little else. Margaret found her comforting to be with. She accepted the gifts with serious approval, propping up the children's drawings on a shelf above her table, putting the loaf of bread into a big covered basket, and then pouring a tin mug of tea for Margaret.

Margaret showed her the bone, placing it on her grandmother's table. To her surprise, the old lady went to a basket against the wall and took out a similar bone. The incisions were different, this one had a bit of crosshatching at one end and a little hole in the other, but they were about the same size.

"This was my drinking tube. We used them when we were girls learning to be women. Our mouths couldn't touch the water, you see, so we had these to drink with, either from a creek or from little bark cups we were given. Mine was a whistle, too," and putting the bone to her lips, she blew a thin, shrill note. A dog outside, maybe Margaret's, began to bark.

"What kind of bone is it, Grandmother?"

"Ah well, we used the crane at Shulus, its leg, I mean. Or sometimes a swan leg, sometimes a goose."

"How old were you?" Margaret wanted to imagine her grandmother, young and smooth-skinned, drinking water through a crane's leg bone.

"It was when we first began the bleeding. We moved away from the others into, well, a hut made with fir boughs. I was fourteen or near enough, and my father made me my hut on a mountainside above the river at Shulus. It was mostly just branches leaning into one another and wrapped at the top with twine made from Indian hemp. My mother and aunties came to help me for part of the time. There were things I couldn't eat and special ways to do things that I had to learn. It was hard work, lots of carrying, digging, running, making my body strong. There was a special headdress to wear, balsam fir, and it hung over my face. I loved the smell, and sometimes I'd take a piece into my mouth and chew it a little. We brushed our bodies with fir, too."

"How long did it take?"

"Oh, quite a time, five moons at least, more for some girls, less for others, but I learned what I needed to know."

Margaret touched her grandmother's arm. "Like what, Grandmother?"

Her grandmother laughed and patted her hand. "Oh, you would think it foolish. When your mother reached her age, the priest wouldn't let her come to us for her lessons. But we learned to make our bodies pure, and how to make baskets and rope, how to prepare ourselves for having children. How to be kind to our friends, how to give, how to keep ourselves from sickness. The name I received was Hidden Root because I learned about plants and could find the potatoes and bitterroot so easily."

"I don't know any of that. I know how to sew, of course, and bake bread, and I know about birds and animals from Father. And the work from school — sums, reading, compositions . . . could you teach me some of what you learned?"

"Margaret, the priests have told us that this is not what God wants us to do. But I never thought He would care about it one way or the other. If I hadn't learned about the plants, how many sick people would have left my door without something to help them? The priests come when someone is dying, yes, but they know nothing about our land and our own medicines. None of the young girls go through the lessons anymore, and I wonder who will remember any of it when the elders are gone. I am too old to take you through the different stages, and I don't think your father and mother would want you to go back to that. But I will tell you some of what I remember. And we will keep making baskets together. That will teach you how to use plants and make something useful."

After tea and a bowl of stew, Margaret and her grandmother gathered some baskets together and followed one of the creeks north of Douglas Lake up into a group of hills bright with spring sunflowers. The old woman told the girl that they'd come to this place every year with their faces painted — "some of us painted our whole face red, some just put a dot on each cheek" — and that they had a prayer:

> I inform you that I intend to eat you,
> may you help me to grow,
> may you help me to be graceful,
> not to be lazy.
> You are the most mysterious of all plants.

"This was our most important plant because we used so many parts of it, and each part had a different name in the old language, the stalk, the root, a different name for a collection of roots, the seeds, a name for when the leaves were just beginning to show. You'd know when other plants would be ready by this one. When the sunflower bloomed, it wouldn't be long for the bitterroot, the spring buds, all the others we used."

"What does it taste like?" Margaret was thinking of the yellow petals and what it would be like to eat flowers.

"We'll bring some back, eh, and you'll know. The roots have to be cooked and then added to the pot of meat or fish. Some grease with it is good." Grandmother Jackson took a knife from one of the baskets and carefully pried up several long tap roots, shaking the dirt from them gently. She then cut the entire crown of a little plant that had not yet flowered for a spring treat. Offering Margaret a part of it, she put the remainder into her mouth and chewed it with pleasure. Margaret chewed cautiously, finding the flavour mild and a little bitter.

"The girls, they made moccasins of the leaves, putting sweet-grass inside, after their first bleeding. Put one of these against your cheek and think what it would feel like to wear the moccasins."

Margaret closed her eyes and felt the fine hairs of the leaves, inhaling the smell, dry and warm, like the hills. She thought hard about the young girls coming away from their people, wanting to feel them around her in the unchanged hills as they learned their place in the landscape, which was her home. Sometimes, when she rode alone beyond the ranch, she had a sense that she was entering a timeless world where everything was of value: the erratics with their cryptic patterns of lichen, long grasses with insects riding their seedheads in the wind, a pile of bear scat alive with seeds containing the knowledge of what they would become — thistle, berry bush, little thorny rose. She would pass through this world quietly, only the soft sound of her horse's hooves on dust, as much a part of it as sky. If she had time, she'd dismount and find a warm patch of grasses to lie among, her horse content to graze, the bit jingling against her teeth. Margaret would will each limb and muscle to relax into grass and go into a kind of sleep, motionless, while the horned larks sang in a tongue she could almost understand. She was weightless, unburdened, her hair perfumed. Rising, she took the memory of grass with her on the rest of her travels, tiny seeds thrust into the warmth of her hair.

Opening her eyes, Margaret returned to her grandmother. "But why was the bone sticking out of the ground? Mother thought it was part of a burial ground when I told her about the rocks all around, but why would a drinking tube be in a burial ground?"

Her grandmother came close and put her arm around the girl's shoulders. "Margaret, when a girl died young, maybe still in the middle of her learning, or even before she began to bleed, she took her things into the grave with her, things she would have needed if she had lived. I think our people were careful to make sure the dead ones went prepared, not knowing what to expect. That drinking tube was buried with a girl, probably there's a digging stick, too, somewhere, still underground — the graves weren't deep then — and her shoes, some beads, a little food. Sometimes even a dog would be buried with its owner. And there are so many reasons why she might have died young."

Margaret was quiet, thinking of the girl beneath the ground on the ridge above Lauder's Creek. Not lying on her back, as though sleeping, but with her knees drawn up to her chin, bound there with bark twine. Had the girl seen the coyote pups leaping and rolling in the dry grass when they first left the den, did she watch the eagles on Hamilton Mountain before it was called that and wonder how it must feel to hang in the air so high and still, did she bury her face in blossoming sage, sneezing as she inhaled the tiny flies that sucked at the nectar? Most of all, was she related to Margaret, through blood down all the generations? And was she afraid to die and leave the world? The Indians at Douglas Lake had believed that the souls lived in a western world, underground. Now that most of them were Christians, it was heaven where the soul went, taken upward on wings, as though by eagles. But Grandmother Jackson still read the stars like an old storybook, saying, "We think of those stars as the children of Black Bear, and we call that the grey trail, the tracks of the dead." When Margaret visited, they'd stand outside the cabin after dark to listen for loons, and Grandmother pointed out the stories of the tribe written across the sky. The moon and his sister, shadows and smoke, the dog following the cluster of stars that William called the Pleiades. When the two women, young and old, stood in the darkness, Margaret thought that she never wanted to leave. She wanted to learn to make baskets and medicines and stay in her grandmother's house forever. Yet it was not quite home.

Margaret's young sisters, Jane and Mary, favoured their father in appearance, having reddish lights in their brown hair and fair skin. Jane's eyes were blue, Mary's a clear grey. When William Stuart's mother and sister from Astoria came to visit, the younger girls hung about them constantly, asking for stories, watching Elizabeth patiently cut and sew the bright calico she had brought into pretty dresses for them, and letting her style their hair into ringlets with rags and an iron rod she heated on the woodstove. Margaret felt shy with the ladies, felt the contrast between their creamy skin and her own darker colouring; she was also wary of their expectations of woman-hood. "A lady never rides astride." "A lady never allows the sun to ruddy her complexion." "Keep your voice soft and low, and always wait to be spoken to." But no matter what Aunt Elizabeth said, you could not ride sidesaddle when you were rounding up cattle. It was important to be able to crouch low when your horse cut out sharply, to grip with your knees, to balance yourself with your stirrups at a lope. And how could you do it in a skirt?

She knew this but felt uncomfortable contradicting her aunt. After all, she knew about the flowers of Grasse and had brushed Margaret's hair so lovingly that the girl had leaned into her and felt the warm glow of family love wash over her along with the scent of lavender. Sometimes she thought of herself as two people, moving between two homes, two families, often under the same roof. She had dreamed of the Astoria ladies for many weeks after they'd left, seeing herself ride with Aunt Elizabeth in a strange saddle that must have been a gift from her aunt, wearing a long divided skirt and pretty black boots. Her hair had been braided and wrapped around her head in a coronet, satin ribbons woven among the dark strands. Waking, she felt a loss so deep she cried into her pillow. She wondered about the girl in the dream, not quite herself but someone she might almost have been.

The girl on the ridge, under the ground: Margaret wondered if she'd ridden, had a special pony she'd recognize in a herd from a distance, the familiar sheen of sunlight on the flank, the whiskery feel of her lips against her hand as she fitted on a bridle.

But she supposed there hadn't always been horses here in the valley. And certainly the girl wore buckskin, unless she was very poor; then she'd have worn a robe of willow or sage bark. Maybe she had died of influenza. This past winter, when the younger children had been so sick, Mother and Father had told her that they must be prepared for the possibility of losing one of them. There had been high fevers and delirium, and Mother had worked so hard to keep the children comfortable, making broth and plain puddings, cooling their heads with cloths soaked in spring water. Margaret had tried to think of what life on the ranch would be like without their voices, their presence at the long table, the girls giggling in bed at night in their shared room.

A gravestone in the graveyard at St. Andrews Church had always haunted Margaret. It was white stone with a carving at the top, a woman lying down with her left arm cradling a baby. Underneath was written: *In affectionate remembrance of Mary Ann Whitford, beloved wife of Samuel Moore. Born 31 Oct'r 1855, Died 13 Oct'r 1881 also infant dau. Mary Agnes Moore, Died 31 Oct'r 1881, aged 19 days.* That meant the mother died one day after her baby had been born, and the child died on her mother's birthday. Margaret wondered if anything sadder had ever happened to anyone and how the father went on living. When she realized that the father was the Samuel Moore who lived at Beaver Ranch — he'd died of old age when Margaret was about ten — she felt sadder still. That house must have been haunted with the ghost of the exhausted mother, having carried her baby for so long only to die before she had a chance to know the wee thing, and the ghost of the babe, taken to be with its mother in heaven, leaving the father with his hope and love departed. In 1881, her own father was still in Astoria, not even knowing this valley existed. Two years later, he was working on the Thompson Plateau, six years later he'd met and married her mother, seven and a half years later, Margaret herself had been born in the tiny cabin that the cowhands now slept in. That little girl born in 1881 would have been a woman now, someone

Margaret would certainly have known; she'd have seen her at the entertainments, at church, community picnics, perhaps even accompanied her to Kamloops for dress materials as she had Mrs. Lauder. Some days it was too much to fathom, how a year could pass and leave so much change and sorrow in its wake and such tremendous happiness, too. And to imagine her life any different, a father who hadn't come north through Washington territory, a different mother, a grandmother who didn't live in a log house near the shore of Douglas Lake with an osprey nest in her tallest tree.

And now the knowledge of this young girl, at the threshold of womanhood, lost to her family, bound in the earth with her digging stick of antler, her medicine bag, a necklace of elk teeth. Margaret could see her, almost, an outline fading in and out of view, a shadow in the tall grass which parted and rustled as she passed. Who would she have become? Grandmother had told Margaret that mothers used to take their babies in their buckskin sacks laced to the cradleboard to the digging ground with them, and, after the mother had painted her own face, she danced before the infant all night, praying to the mountains and other spirits that evil and sickness might never come to her child. When the child had outgrown the cradleboard, it was hung in a tree a distance from the village site and not used again for any other child. Margaret wondered about this girl's cradleboard: perhaps birds had taken away the buckskin, the hairs of the blanket made of fawn skin, perhaps mice had nested in the remains. So much could go wrong in a life, even if all the measures were taken in time.

Margaret had not had much formal schooling. The school was down in the community of Nicola Lake, too far to ride to every day. She'd gone for a week at a time some spring and autumn months, staying with a family, the Pooleys occasionally, the Howses, doing her sums by lamplight at night at the round table in the Pooley's parlour. She loved reading, everything from the new *Nicola Herald* to the family Bible; the words made such a clear picture sometimes, staying in her memory like photographs. When God spoke to Job out of the whirlwind, when He asked, *Hast thou entered into the treasures of the snow? or has thou seen the treasures of the hail?*, Margaret could see the opening into the blizzard that God certainly meant, and surely He himself had seen the summer ground covered with hailstones all glittering and cold, looking like Culloden after a storm. And once Reverend Murray had read the sixty-fifth psalm in church, and she thought she would swoon with the loveliness of the picture: *Thou waterest the ridges thereof abundantly: thou settlest the furrows thereof: thou makest it soft with showers: thou blessest the springing thereof. . . . The pastures are clothed with flocks, the valleys also are covered over with corn; they shout for joy, they also sing.* It was as though God was speaking of her own ranch, the beauty of the hayfields ripe with grass, and the music of the yellow-headed blackbirds in the marsh.

When she was staying with the Howses one spring, in their big house across from the church, there had been an entertainment in the hotel and a number of people sang or played the piano or recited poetry. One man, a visitor at Quilchena, recited a sonnet by Mr. William Shakespeare, and Margaret never forgot it, especially the way the man had said each word slowly and dramatically, even sighing after the first line, *From you have I been absent in the spring,* so that you could feel the longing of the poet for his love.

> *Nor did I wonder at the lily's white,*
> *Nor praise the deep vermilion in the rose;*
> *They were but sweet, but figures of delight,*
> *Drawn after you, you pattern of all those.*

The room was quiet after the conclusion of the poem, as though everyone there was putting a face to the object of the poet's longing. Margaret copied out that poem later from the volume of Shakespeare at school and kept it in her Bible at home so that she could feel again the shiver of delight the words created in her, the sweet sadness of the feeling, although she had no face to praise or long for.

When we sat by our campfire at night, I could almost hear voices, but listen as I might, hard as I could, I could never make out what they were saying. It was enough to almost hear them, I thought, feeling the deep heartbeat of the ponderosa pines in the ground below our tent. When the moon was right, there was a path of moonlight from our camp to Quilchena. And all around, the grass turned obscure in the darkness, no longer gilded with endless skies of sunlight or shadowed by high tumbling cloud.

> *This grass is very dark to be from the white heads*
> *of old mothers.*
> *Darker than the colourless beards of old men,*
> *Dark to come from under the faint red roofs of mouths.*

Sometimes I looked at the crescent of houses on the road in to the campsite and thought about buying one. I wanted a way to locate ourselves in the dry soil of the Nicola Valley, a place to dream about when elsewhere, a site to venture from on exploratory drives up over that hill or along the road following the river west to Spences Bridge. But it wasn't this time that I felt drawn to, not the trim Lindal houses with their gardens of saucer-sized dahlias and their squares of watered lawn. It was more to an interval, maybe only a decade or two, when the community of Nicola Lake thrived, complete with grist mill and sawmill, bakery, laundry, harness shops and livery, banks and the courthouse, newspaper office and hotels. Sometimes I try to dream my way back to those busy streets, perhaps a girl on a compact bay mare, on her way to watch her father play polo against the Kamloops team.

It was as though we had known each other all our lives and had just been reunited after a long absence . . .

And sometimes the thought of never having lived here, never having come to womanhood in these dry hills, stabs at my heart like a thin knife, piercing me with such longing that I am breathless. I have dreamed of a girl and, waking, inhale particles of dust that might have contained her, the seeds of tender grass, the feathery hairs of her horse's fetlock. A girl who might almost have existed, a life that might almost have occurred, everywhere and always.

A photograph of a girl with smaller children, her sisters and brother, dressed as though for church. They are standing in a yard of some sort, fence rails in evidence, a barn in the distance. The girls are all in sprigged dresses, ankle length for the oldest and below the knee for the two younger, pleated bodices edged in narrow lace, cuffs buttoned to the elbow. The boy is wearing a Norfolk jacket and short pants. They are smiling for the camera while behind them a grove of cottonwoods casts textured shadow on the sunlit yard, a rope swing dangles from one tall branch, and off to one side a line of sheets pauses, too, for the photographer's eye, as if to tell the viewer that this family, posed for eternity in their Sunday best, also climbed trees, slept in beds with wind-dried linens wrapping them in an intimate embrace.

This reminds me of my growing collection of textiles for the exhibition, how bed linens are so rarely saved and cherished. Yet one pillowcase has come to me, its edge beautifully hem-stitched and with an intricate monogram in French whitework embroidery, two initials entwined like vines, D and R, around a central M, with exquisitely worked satin stitch flowers and leaves. The fabric is very thin and fine and will need careful treatment for display. But what impresses me most is not its handwork but the knowledge that it was almost certainly intended for a marriage, that lovers might have slept with their heads close upon it. If only there was a way to decode the memories contained in cottons and woollens, buckskin and beadwork, the shape of bodies impressed in fibres.

Chapter Four

THE ITEMS ACCUMULATE as I hoped they would. The little jacket's mystery is becoming clear; two Japanese families lived in my community until the War. One of the men was a boatbuilder, and their home was confiscated by authorities and resold to a local family. When I ask about them, I am told about his skill, shown boats that were his design. "And did she sew?" I ask the oldest women, and someone almost remembers that she did. So the jacket might have been a gift or a hand-me-down. I spend some time looking at examples of Japanese quilting, admiring the practicality — padded jackets were made for firemen and farmers in handsome dark blue cotton, the tiny white stitches making them strong enough to withstand many washings. And even earlier, the padding was used to make a kind of armour, channels filled with pieces of horn or metal. The *shibori* dye patterns are fascinating, too — *ne maki*, thread-resist rings, and *mokume*, woodgrain. The impulse to look at the natural world, all its cycles and phenomena, and to mirror these patterns in textiles is a thread of history that pulls me to follow it to the heart of a maze.

And, as well, I am taking the unravelled threads from a life and trying to reweave a companion piece, not the life itself but its image.

May 13, 1906: The Douglas Plateau

From her eastern window under the gable, muslin curtain drawn back by the breeze, Margaret could see morning opening upon the home fields, mauve, pale pink, a faint orange like the opened belly of a trout, gold and dove grey. A few tendrils of honeysuckle ventured in the open window, and a blackbird's piercing whistle. It was too lovely to stay in bed and too early for anyone else to be up and about. She left her bed, pulling up the warm sheets and her quilt with its border of wild geese, and quickly put on her clothing.

Out the door, out to the barn to change into her blessed trousers in the tack-room graced by a coyote skull over the lintel, grabbing a bridle and a tin of oats. Daisy was standing under a cottonwood with the blue roan gelding, and Margaret gave them each a handful of oats, leading Daisy away to be saddled by the barn. She wanted to be up on the ridge before the sun came over, wanted to see the darkened windows flare. It was a Sunday, and everyone was taking an hour or two of extra rest, even the ranch dogs lying on the porch. One of them barked a little as Margaret led Daisy through the gate and then returned to sleep.

Daisy was fresh and sidestepped as Margaret tried to mount; once up, she tightened the reins as the mare snorted and blew, wanting to run. Margaret gave her the chance on the lower slope of the ridge, letting her gallop until she slowed down as the hill grew steeper, sweet oaten breath drifting back to her rider's face. Once on the summit, Margaret dismounted to look back at the ranch as the sun came up. Everything was illuminated, house, summer kitchen, barn, bunkhouse, by clean sunlight. A rooster crowed once, then again for the sound of his own voice. Seeing her home from this vantage gave Margaret a sharp delicious ache, as though she was watching the life of the ranch go on without her. As though she had never been part of it, watching from the years ahead while the trees grew to shelter her absence. Mounting again, she rode east, letting Daisy gallop along the ridge, the smell of young southernwood rising from her hooves.

She decided to ride to the spring range to see if there were messages to take home to her father. The cowhands were camped in a shack they'd fixed up, their bedrolls stretched out on plank bunks, a stone fireplace outside to bake biscuits and grill slabs of marbled beef. An old coffee pot frothed continuously on the back of the fire, the cook adding water until the cowhands refused to drink the bitter brew; then he'd rinse the pot in a cursory sort of way in the nearby creek and start fresh. They were pleased with this cook, a Celestial who'd come recommended from Douglas Lake last year. He had an odd smell, sort of sweet and tarry; Margaret's father told her it was opium, which the Celestials smoked. She found the little jars sometimes when she helped to clean up the camp after the cowhands had moved on to a new range and was fascinated by the writing on them, more like the marks on her grandmother's baskets than the alphabet she knew. And once she found a tin with a rooster on its label. Opening it, she could smell the cook's fingers as he handed her a plate of food, his clothing.

As Margaret rode, she was thinking of the treat in store for her family. Her father had purchased tickets for concert in Kamloops; Madame Emma Albani was coming to the Opera House with several other singers, and Father had booked rooms at the Grand Pacific Hotel. They were going by stage — the Costleys ran stages in summer, fall and spring, and a horse-drawn sleigh in winter — and were making a holiday of it. Father knew Angus Nelson, the rider for the stable, from the days when the Kamloops hockey team came to play at Nicola Lake. Angus had been both team captain and a forward during the last game at the Kamloops rink; Margaret's father had played goal for Nicola. That was 1902, and every year since then, both men hoped to organize more games. They'd meet on the Kamloops-Forksdale road, William Stuart taking harness into Nicola Lake to be mended or planning to look at a horse at Pooley's, Angus

Nelson stopping the stage briefly to discuss the possibility of matches for the upcoming winter. It was Angus who told William about Madame Albani's concert: "You'll not have the chance again, Stuart. She has a stop-over en route to a concert in Vancouver, and she's giving this concert as a kindness, really. Bring the family, why don't you? You and I could meet for a drink at the Inland Club and talk about next winter."

Margaret had never attended any function at the Opera House. She'd seen the building on trips to Kamloops and loved its facade, imagining the opulent interior. She would wear her deep rose muslin dress and the pearls Father had given her for her sixteenth birthday. Musing and dreaming, she rode on until Daisy stopped in her tracks and nickered softly.

Three men sat under a ponderosa; one of them she recognized as George Edwards, who worked, as far as she knew, at the Douglas Lake ranch. He rose and walked toward her, holding his palm flat for Daisy to sniff.

"It's Stuart's girl, isn't it? I've seen you with your dad. Where are you bound for?"

(From my distance ahead of her, waiting in history, I want to tell her, Yes, take pleasure in pearls, yes, show kindness to acquaintances and strangers taking the morning air under a patterned shadow of pines.)

"Yes, I recognize you, Mr. Edwards. I'm going to our spring range, to see if there's anything the men need. It was too nice when I woke up to do anything but saddle my horse and think of somewhere to ride."

She'd always liked George Edwards. He played fiddle sometimes at the socials, and he often had candy for children he met.

People said he'd been a cobbler, and in fact he made shoes for some of the poorest families in the area, never charging them anything. It was odd to see him away from Douglas Lake, though. As if he read her thoughts, he said, "I'm not working for Greaves anymore. There was an accident with the irrigation team, some Chinaman thought I'd killed his brother and threatened to poison me. And who can blame him if he really believed I was responsible, though I wasn't. But Joe and I thought I should make myself scarce, so I'm doing a little prospecting now with Shorty, here, and Louis. We've got our eye on a creek over towards Tulameen. Here you go, young lady, something to sweeten your ride."

Mr. Edwards handed her a peppermint stick, a swirl of red and white stripes, and she tucked it into her pocket for later. The other two men nodded to her and began gathering up their gear. She waved goodbye and went on her way, thinking how nice Mr. Edwards was, how gentle his eyes under the brim of his hat, which he'd raised to her as if she were a grown woman. She liked to listen to his drawl, and when he sang "My Old Kentucky Home" there were always tears.

The next morning was overcast, some rain and then periods when the billowing clouds parted enough to let the sun through. In the higher parts of the plateau, on Hamilton Mountain, for instance, it would be snowing, the clouds shaking down gusts of it to dust the new flowers and grass. When Margaret's father asked her to take some pinkeye medicine for the new calves to the spring camp, she readily agreed. Daisy had returned home from yesterday's ride with a bruised frog as a result of picking up a sharp pebble in her hoof, so Margaret saddled the blue roan gelding, a bigger and stronger mount. Like Daisy, he was very fresh and wanted to run. They finished the errand quickly, and Margaret decided to take the longer way home, around Chapperon Lake, to see if the cranes had returned to the marsh at the end of the lake. She loved to watch them flying on the thermals in a V like geese but then dispersing in the warm air, gathering again in formation as they met the next current. Sometimes there would be nearly a hundred in flight, though only about ten pairs nested on the marsh. They were beautiful birds, graceful in flight and attentive to their young. She couldn't imagine hunting them, though her mother's people must have done so. She wondered if they tasted like goose, which was delicious. In hunting season her father shot ducks and geese and returned home with strings of them hanging behind his saddle. She hated plucking them because they had to be singed, a disgusting job, but then Mother roasted some with stuffings of apples, dried serviceberries and onions and preserved a few in their own fat to flavour soups in winter.

The terrain near Chapperon Lake was rocky, wooded with tall firs and aspens and, in the draws near water, slender willows and cottonwoods. The gelding was sure-footed, and Margaret was not paying much attention when suddenly he shied to the left, almost unseating her. Ahead, perhaps a hundred feet, she could see a little wisp of smoke rising from behind a low, brushy hill. A mounted rider gestured to a party of men to close ranks behind him. They all dismounted and stepped slowly into the brush. Realizing that she hadn't been seen, Margaret slid down from her saddle and tied the gelding to a tree. She walked quietly towards the smoke, and when she could see the fire it came from, she slipped behind a tree. To her surprise, the men around the campfire were Mr. Edwards and his companions. One of the strangers asked them where they'd come from.

"Across the river," George Edwards replied. He explained that they'd been prospecting, his voice calm and soft.

The stranger said, "You answer the description of the train robbers we are hunting for, and I arrest you for that crime."

Margaret nearly cried out, "No, you've got it all wrong, that's Mr. Edwards, we all know him, he plays the fiddle," but something, a keen fear, made her return to her horse as Mr. Edwards replied, "Well, we don't look much like train robbers, do we?" She quickly untied the gelding, jumped into the saddle and moved away as quietly as she could. All of a sudden there was shouting — "Look out boys, it's all up" — and then gunshots, many of them, and a man screamed, "I'm shot!"

Margaret pressed her heels into the gelding's sides and urged him to gallop as fast as he could. Her heart was pounding so hard she couldn't catch her breath, but she didn't dare pull her horse up until she reckoned she was a mile or two away. When she finally let the gelding stop, he was lathered with sweat, and she was trembling so hard she had to dismount and sit down in the new grass to calm herself, not caring if it was wet with the day's rain.

Closing her eyes, she saw the strangers sneaking towards Mr. Edwards's camp, heard the stern voice of the one who accused the three of being train robbers, Mr. Edwards's calm, friendly reply. She heard the shots, echoes making it impossible to tell whether there'd been three shots or thirty, the scream, the shouting and chaos in the grove of trees. Her horse's eyes had shown white when she'd mounted him, snapped at his rump with her glove so he took off in a scuffle of dust and mud, kicked him to a gallop. Unshod, his feet had pounded the ground without the ringing of metal shoe on rock. She opened her eyes again and got up to make sure he hadn't chipped a hoof or injured an ankle. He was quiet, standing beside her while she felt his legs, lifting each foot to examine it; she heard his tail swish away the flies and felt his breath on the back of her neck as he turned to see what she was doing. She tried to figure out what she'd seen, what had happened to Mr. Edwards. Was it he who had screamed out that he was shot? Was there anyone she should tell? She wondered if she'd been seen by the strangers, but as no one had followed her, she assumed she hadn't. She decided to ride home right away, the day ruined by the unexpected brutality in the brush near the cranes' marsh.

I have dreamed of a girl bent at the waist to make herself low on her horse's neck. Particles of dust in the dream, strong sweat, long cry of cranes across the pastures. Those men under the pines will be remembered — stern faces looking into a camera lens, broken boots, a worn felt hat. In the memory of a girl, riding in search of wild birds, will linger the image of three men sitting in calm air, a battered coffee pot aslant on a piece of stone. A place that might still hold the mystery of shouts and gunshot, the silenced cranes on the edge of water. Where clouds passing over the bodies of the hills might contain the smoke of their cooking fire.

At the ranch, there were several men in the yard, talking to her father while the sheets snapped and blew in the wind. One man was saying, "They know where the scoundrels are, more or less, they've found tracks, and I'd say they'll get them any time now."

William Stuart called Margaret to him. "I should never have sent you over to the camp this morning. Bill Miner and his gang are on the loose, I didn't hear until now that they robbed a train over at Ducks last week and have been spotted up by Campbell's Meadow. The tracks show them heading over towards Minnie Lake. Go now and take the saddle off that horse, and then I want you to stay close to home until they're caught. A search party is out now with Indian trackers, so it shouldn't be long."

Margaret said nothing. Walking the gelding over to the corral, she began to tremble again. She knew that she couldn't tell her father what she'd seen, thank goodness she hadn't remembered to tell him at dinner last night about seeing George Edwards and his companions. But he liked Mr. Edwards, so why was she relieved not to have told him? It was all so confusing. Was the man Mr. Edwards called Shorty or the one introduced as Louis really the train robber Bill Miner? Why were those men shooting, and who had screamed? One thing she knew for certain: if her father knew she had been where men were shooting, he'd never let her ride alone again.

William saddled up his own horse and headed out with the other men, asking Margaret to milk the cow in his absence. They were headed over to Douglas Lake to see if they could help with the search. Each carried a rifle slung over his shoulder, and Margaret saw her father tuck his Colt into his jacket pocket. She shivered to think of her father in danger and then shivered again to remember how close she'd been to danger herself.

In the house, her mother was clearing up after what had obviously been an interrupted dinner. Her father's plate still held a portion of roast beef and a mound of mashed potatoes.

"Let me get you something to eat, Margaret. You must be hungry."

"No, Mother, I'm fine. I ate a big breakfast and took some bread along on the ride. I'll help you with this."

The routine of clearing plates, stacking them, putting food away helped to settle her heart and mind. She worked hard at the chores for what remained of the afternoon, taking out dinner leavings for the pigs and making sure the horses all had water. She ate supper with her sisters and brother and washed their dishes when they'd finished. At dusk her father was still not back, and so she took out a scalded bucket and milked the Jersey cow who provided milk for the household. Leaning her cheek against the cow's warm flank soothed her as she squeezed each teat, felt the warm fluid as it left the cow's body, listened to the ping against the side of the bucket. Margaret strained the milk, cleaned the bucket and put the jug in the cellar to cool. Already the cream was collecting on the surface; by morning her mother would skim off a full third of the jugful for butter.

Back in the kitchen, Jenny Stuart was sewing by lamplight. Margaret took up a shirt of her father's from the mending basket and began to turn the collar so the frayed part would be underneath. By the time they heard hoofbeats in the yard and the chorus of barking, it was almost completely dark outside.

William called to the ranch dogs to quiet down. He came in, bringing with him a gust of cool air, and he carefully put his rifle away.

"Well, they got the men all right, but you'll never guess who Bill Miner turns out to be. George Edwards! You know him, Margaret, from Douglas Lake? And Jenny, you remember his fiddle playing? Imagine that. I thought for certain they'd made a mistake, but Corporal Wilson from Kamloops is positive this is Miner because of some tattoos. They've gone over to Quilchena for the night to get Doctor Tuthill to look at the one who was shot."

"One was shot?" Margaret asked, wondering which man had screamed so horribly and if he was still alive.

"A fellow called Dunn. Not seriously, though, just a flesh wound to the leg. I can't get over old Edwards, for the life of me. A decent man. We all said that over at Douglas Lake when the Royal North West Mounted Police brought them in. Greaves was the most surprised, didn't believe it at first. I think maybe I don't still. Is there a chance of some supper, Jenny?"

Jenny quickly got her husband a plate of cold beef and pickle, a couple of biscuits, and a wedge of cheese. She poured him a glass of milk from the pitcher she kept cool on the window sill. With his feet on the fender of the big range, he told them about seeing the trio brought in to the home ranch at Douglas Lake, exclaiming every few minutes that he found it hard to believe that Edwards was a train robber. He was too polite for that, surely. And the one other fellow, the one that hadn't been shot, he was so well-spoken, more like a banker than a criminal.

Under her wild geese quilt that night, Margaret dreamed of the three men being herded to Quilchena by a posse of gunslingers and woke in a panic about her own role in the event. Should she have told her father about seeing the shoot-out by the lake? She decided in the moonlight that her father would only worry, and she was safe, wasn't she, so why trouble him with the information? No, this would be a secret between her and the blue roan gelding, and he wouldn't talk, of that she was certain.

I am between two worlds. At my desk in the museum, collating pages or making detailed notes on the items that are brought in to me, my mind wanders along the road winding up behind Quilchena, a road I have driven on to find myself among horses. Outside my window, the dense coastal vegetation obliterates the sky. A quilt, neatly folded in a box, waits for me to examine it. Early in the month I woke from a dream of three men, bent under the weight of provisions, walking across the high grasslands. There was such silence in the grass and overhead a sky like a book of hours, blue and open. In the dream I was a girl again, alone under the sky, waiting for my life to begin, waiting for the pages to turn. And now, well underway, I am left to wonder about the men, the girl, their landscape of sage, pine, soft grasses and wild clematis. Back and forth I move, between home and the valley, my work and this deep exploration of place, the years of my girlhood and the present, between the life of the body and what remains, a few objects, a tube of bone on a rocky hill. Across the hills the men made their way, a girl watching them in secrecy, while on the marshy shores of a lake, cranes nested with their young, oblivious.

And what of the woman I leave when I take the road high above Quilchena? Does she continue on, unchanged, sorting through a box of leavings, wondering about the propriety of reading letters addressed to another? Of preparing marriage linens to be viewed by a generation that never embroidered the initials of lovers into fine cotton? Did anyone know that by such things lives are remembered?

Thinking makes me heavy with loss. I think of Sappho, sur-rounded by young women, and I understand the wistfulness of her lyrics.

> *The night is now*
> *half-gone; youth*
> *goes; I am*
>
> *in bed alone*

Chapter Five

THE OLD ROAD FROM Nicola to Kamloops winds through grassy hills which take your breath away in their stillness. Past Stump Lake, Napier Lake, Trapp Lake, Ussher Lake, unseen in the west but remembered for the murder of John Tannatt Ussher by the sad McLean gang in 1879, past sway-backed cabins collapsing gently into fields, fields alive with savannah sparrows, horned larks, coyotes, through Rose Hill and Knutsford, until it finally leads you into Kamloops itself. Each rise and fall of grass slope is like a basket, a coiled burden basket of split root, hooked through with the bark of bitter cherry, the bleached stems of canary grass. The road a handle, a scaffolding, holding the baskets together with their contents of berries, freckled meadowlark eggs, the occasional horse pausing in its grazing. Driving, we are quiet, thinking of the cattle who passed over this ground, the home-steads forged by those paying the ten-dollar fee under the Dominion Homestead Regulations and then building a house, breaking the land, fencing their quarter section. The maps are quilted with the neat stitches of fencelines, threaded with creeks where stock might wander to drink — Campbell, Peterson, Anderson — and jewelled with lakes, blackbirds whistling from the reeds. In old dooryards are lilacs and roses gone wild; lines of Lombardy poplars remember their planting. A girl born in this landscape would know the wind's quiet voice in the cottonwood leaves and would stop to listen to skeins of geese coming from the south to land on the sloughs. In such ways the world is remembered.

Nicola to Kamloops, May 15-18, 1906

Two days later, the family was waiting for the stage at the Forksdale-Kamloops road. After breakfast, Jenny's brother August had brought them down from the ranch in the buggy, and he would take care of the home ranch while they were away. Jenny and Margaret waited in the buggy while the younger children watched for the stage and William and August talked about the Miner capture. It was all anyone talked about these days. Many felt that a mistake had been made, that a genial man like George Edwards couldn't possibly be the notorious train robber the police insisted he was. They were awaiting positive identification by a Pinkerton detective, but his tattoos gave him away, or so the Corporal had told the men at Douglas Lake. A ballet dancer around his right arm, two stars on his left arm, and a heart pierced with two daggers. There was also a bluebird on his hand. These marks had not been noteworthy among the native people in the Nicola area because the Thompsons often tattooed themselves in connection with important dreams or to inspire courage and strength.

The stage announced itself in a cloud of dust, four bay horses at a brisk trot. It drew up, and the horses stood still while the Stuart family said their goodbyes to August. William's friend Angus Nelson was driving, so after tying the luggage securely onto the roof, the two men sat on the driver's bench with Tom in the middle; Tom held the reins proudly on the straight stretches of road. Jenny, Margaret and the two girls were tucked inside, Mary and Jane holding on to the edges of their seats for dear life. Jenny looked nervous. Margaret was beginning to understand that her mother was happiest at home with her own children around for company or with other ranch families whom she knew well. She would go with the family to concerts and outings, but she seemed uncomfortable in large groups or in unfamiliar settings. Once Margaret had observed a woman speaking quietly to another as the Stuart family arrived at a Victoria Day fete in Nicola Lake, and she overheard one woman say "klootchie" and nod significantly at Jenny Stuart. Later Margaret asked her father privately what the term meant. Furious, he told her never to use such a word in the presence of her mother, that it was meant to demean Indian women, like squaw, and he would not hear it used in reference to his wife or any other woman.

"But Father, I only asked you because I didn't know, I'd never heard it until the women at the picnic —"

William pulled her to him. "Margaret, I'm sorry, I know you weren't being disrespectful. There's an attitude, though, you will come upon it in your life, possibly you already have, that distinguishes between Indians and whites. It's hypocritical, you know, especially in this valley where a lot of the families have intermarried — look at the Coutlees and Voghts. I love your mother, and I won't have her hurt. And, my dear, that goes for you as well. You are as good as anyone alive, you have the blood of the Stuart kings in your veins as well as noble Thompson blood. Keep your head high, and don't let the small souls of the world hurt your feelings."

In the box of her life, a length of bone, some photographs, a program. How do I balance the composition of what might be expected of a young woman of her time and place with what might be remarkable? What have I learned from dreaming her shape into my life, and how can I know what is memory and what is desire? *One person struck by a stone*, said Pliny, *forgot solely how to read and write. Another who fell from a very high roof forgot*

71

his mother. And as sleep gradually steals over one, it restricts the
memory and causes the inactive mind to wonder where it is. But
what if the mind has not forgotten, exactly, but has remembered
a girl who might never have been? Not a mother, not a sister, but
a younger earlier self? What if the mind carries her as imagery of
nostalgia, which is only a longing for home? And what is home
but the cradle of the self? Carried in the wild rye, the bunchgrass, the yellow feathers of rabbitbrush, in soft wind, the subtle
seeds pause and attach.

Thinking on what her father had said, Margaret remembered
a certain coolness on the part of some of the girls at school, but
she'd put that down to the fact that she didn't attend regularly
and hadn't made friends as easily as the others. And there had
been lots of children who were either fully Indian or who had
one Indian parent. Oddly, Margaret had never really thought
about this before in any meaningful way. She was who she was,
they were who they were. Sometimes you liked a person, found
her congenial, sometimes you had nothing in common. Many
were eager for male attention and talked endlessly of who was
sweet on whom and whether their affection was returned. Little
tokens were exchanged carefully, so the teacher wouldn't catch
on. Margaret had never received a token from a boy or a girl, nor
had she given one. Because she came to school infrequently, she
was intent on learning as much as she could while she was
there. She couldn't remember taunts specific to her Indian
blood, though. Or would she have recognized a taunt if she
heard one?

None of it mattered this fine May morning on the road to
Kamloops, but it did make Margaret feel a protective tenderness
toward her mother, and she linked her arm through Jenny's and
put her head on her mother's shoulder. Her mother patted her
hair with one gloved hand. Jenny Stuart wore a dark blue gabar-

dine skirt she'd made that winter and a jacket of soft grey wool. At home she never wore a hat, but for the trip she'd trimmed her navy straw boater with a piece of grey velvet ribbon. It was soothing to sit by her and smell both the unaccustomed fragrance of clothing stored in a cedar-lined trunk and the familiar scent of her hair and skin.

The ride to Kamloops took twelve hours. The usual stage from Forksdale was spread over two days, but Angus Nelson told William he was trying a one-day run, and this fit nicely with William's plans. Stops were made along the way, one to change horses at Rockford on Stump Lake, where tea and hot biscuits were provided. Later, Angus stopped to water the team as needed at lakes near the road; he untied a bucket from under his seat and dipped it into the cold water, letting each horse drink its fill. Everyone stretched their legs and disappeared behind bushes to relieve themselves on the warm ground. It was a beautiful drive, the road rising high and passing hill after hill of blowing grass. Marshes alive with blackbirds could be seen as the horses clipped along, and once Tom called out for them to see coyotes at play in the sunshine.

It was growing dark when they arrived in Kamloops, but the city was vibrant with life. The stage took them directly to the Grand Pacific Hotel, its entrance on the corner of Fourth Avenue and Lansdowne Street lit by a street lamp. The manager was expecting them and directed a boy to take their bags up to the suite of rooms Father had reserved. The children were thrilled to see that the window of their room opened onto a balcony overlooking the street. They kept calling one another to see the lively scene below — two men laughing loudly as they left the hotel's saloon; a Chinese family hurrying in another direction, the mother dressed in bright clothing and walking in small steps behind the father; a group of men seated under the trees outside the hotel talking of the Miner gang. Phrases of their conversation rose up to the family leaning out the window, screened by darkness and the new leaves. Father explained that the train robbers were being held in the Kamloops prison awaiting their trial on May 28. The manager, who had come up to make sure all was in order, told him that he was lucky he'd booked the rooms early. Now, what with Madame Albani's concert and the Miner trial, most hotels were full to the brim. People were coming from as far away as Vancouver to attend the trial and to get a glimpse of the notorious Bill Miner.

"He may be the fella, all right, but I hear over and over again that George Edwards wouldn't hurt a fly, everyone likes him, and there seem to be irregularities about his arrest. They say the Pinkerton detective, a weasely sort called Seavey, led him to believe he was an attorney. False pretences, I say, and so say many others, too. Ah, Stuart, you'll find this town fairly buzzing."

It was difficult to get to sleep that first night in Kamloops. The beds were unfamiliar, the pillows deep and soft. Margaret woke in darkness and couldn't get her bearings. Where she was accustomed to seeing the moon through a lattice of ponderosa directly in front of her bed, there was a wall. Then she remembered where she was; she could hear her parents talking quietly in the other room, which reassured her, and she sank back into the pillows to make the morning come sooner.

I have slept in old hotels, not the Grand Pacific (famous for its bathrooms, among the first in Kamloops), which burned in the thirties, but others, in Paris, in Dublin, in the Nicola Valley itself. I know she listened to the creak of timbers beyond the dark ceilings as the building adjusted its weight, the sound of pulleys, the quiet voices of the kitchen help at first light, taking a moment to enjoy a smoke before beginning their day. And the peach-skin softness of the sheets in their folds, the smell of soap and the wind of Kamloops, a different wind from the one she was accustomed to, bringing with it train fumes and commerce and the faint odour of the North Thompson tumbling from its headwaters down through Avola, Clearwater, McLure. All over Kamloops while she slept, the city waited for morning. In the jail, the three accused robbers slept fitfully; in the Fulton household, the family of the Attorney General dreamed of his successful prosecution of Bill Miner, still to come; in the newspaper offices, the typesetters wiped inky hands on their aprons and held up chases of type to place in the presses, pulling a proof of the headlines, excited at playing a small part in history. And on the road from the Cherry Creek ranch, a hopeful wrangler rode a pretty bay mare at a quick trot, not wanting to miss an appointment with William Stuart.

Rising before the others, Margaret went to the window in her nightdress to look out at the street. Sounds of the morning filled the air — a rooster, even in the city, crowed the hour; buckets clanging in the livery stable told her that horses were being fed; a boy carried newspapers down the street and dropped them at many of the doorsteps, including the hotel's. Two men in suits were striding down the road, and one looked up to see her in the window, her shoulders bare and her hair still unbrushed. He raised his hat and called out to her — she was a lovely sight to behold this fine May morning. Margaret's hands flew to her face and she left the window in a hurry, her cheeks burning. By now the children were stirring, and she could hear her father cough. She put her clothes on and went down the hall to use the bathroom. A maid just coming out the door told her that the towels were fresh, and there was lots of hot water should she care to bathe. What luxury, thought Margaret, as she ran a tub of water and stretched out in comfort. At home, they heated water for baths on the stove and then emptied the tub, bucket by bucket, after. But this was lovely, hot water up to her chin, and then big towels to dry off with as the water ran down the drain, whirling like an eddy on the Nicola River. She returned to the suite of rooms to find her family waiting for her so they could go down for breakfast.

A table had been set for them, and a newspaper was folded beside the plate William Stuart sat to. He unfolded it, shook out the wrinkles and read the headline aloud: THE CHASE, CAPTURE AND THE COMMITTAL. A waitress served coffee to William and Jenny and looked inquiringly at Margaret, who started to demur but then impulsively held out her cup. The newspapers made the capture of George Edwards seem heroic, she thought, as though a dangerous criminal had been caught at great risk to the team of men and dogs who had tracked them down. She saw again the three men around a campfire preparing a meal, the approach of the posse, the questions, Mr. Edwards's calm replies, and then she heard the sound of gunfire and screams as she galloped away over the spring grass, the meadowlarks silent in the pauses between gunshots. The coffee tasted good, and she breathed in its aroma as she raised the cup to her mouth.

"Margaret, if you're going to drink coffee, you should at least take cream. There's no need to drink it black, as though you're in a cowcamp." Her father smiled and then returned to the newspaper. He didn't stop reading until plates of eggs and slices of pink ham, mounds of potatoes dusted with parsley, and high golden biscuits were placed in front of the family. Margaret thought she couldn't possibly eat such a huge breakfast, but each mouthful tasted wonderful, and before she knew it, her plate was clean. Her brother and sisters, too, had made similar short work of their breakfasts and were eager to be excused to explore the street. Jenny Stuart took them out into the morning after conferring with her husband to find out what plans he had for the day. He told her he'd arranged to meet someone at a stable down the road in order to inspect a mare. He'd take Margaret, if Jenny could spare her, because he wanted her opinion.

Margaret changed her shoes and they walked the short distance to the stable, arriving there before the man they were to meet. William knew the owner and went into the barn with him to see some saddles, and Margaret remained on the bench in front of the stable, reading the newspaper that had been left there. Each player in the capture of the train robbers had a tale to tell — the provincial constable who first met the three near the Stevens ranch and raced back to Douglas Lake for help, the Royal North West Mounted Police sergeant from Calgary who approached the three men by the fire and accused them of the crime. The paper was full of the story from all possible angles, from notes of the preliminary hearing two days earlier to an account of Bill Miner's connection to the Aspen Grove and Nicola Valley communities. Margaret was engrossed in reading every word when her father came out. She tucked the newspaper into her handbag and rose from the bench as her father said, "Margaret, come see this mare. Tell me what you think."

William led her through the barn to some holding pens behind. A bay mare was waiting there, pushing her nose curiously in Margaret's direction. She blew air into the flat palm the girl offered her, then lowered her head to smell Margaret's dress, allowing the girl to stroke her ears and run her hands down the mare's neck to the muscular chest. She removed a twig from the forelock, which was short and brushy, like a thistle. The mare was not big, Margaret judged her to be about fifteen hands, maybe fifteen-one, but she gave an impression of vitality because of her broad chest, strong legs, healthy coat and wide clear eyes.

"She's from Cherry Creek," William explained. "They've got a good breeding program right now, and I'd like to have a purebred mare with her size and strength. I think she'd throw a good foal if we bred her to the Bonny Prince." The Bonny Prince was the stud that William had acquired a few years earlier, a handsome stallion gentle enough to use as a saddle horse. Margaret thought the prospect of a foal from the two was excellent, and she told her father so.

"Her legs look good, Father, no splints or spavins that I can see. Does she mind her feet being held?"

"Why don't we try her?" William climbed over the fence and approached the mare's left side. She looked at him curiously but didn't move, even when he lifted each foot in turn, examining the inner foot for thrush or damage. He ran his hands down her legs to feel for lumps or sensitive areas and was pleased to find none, pleased that the mare stood quietly for this. Putting his fingers in the sides of her mouth, he opened her jaw so that he could examine her teeth. When he'd finished she blew so hard that her lips vibrated, but still she was calm.

The horse's handler, sensing that a deal was imminent, went into the barn to leave William and Margaret alone.

"I think we'll take her, Margaret. What do you think?"

"She's lovely, Father. Do you intend to ride her home?"

William had thought about this and wondered how best to do it. "She's not in foal now, they weaned her last colt a few months ago, and she's in good condition, I'd say. What about you riding her along with the stage to the stopping house at Trapp Lake, then continuing home in the stage with the others? I'll stay overnight at Trapp Lake and finish the journey the next day. I don't want to strain her; it would be better to keep her pace a little slower than the stage's, I think."

"But Father, I've nothing to ride in. I didn't bring clothes I could wear to ride all that way."

William looked at his daughter, cleared his throat once, then twice. "Margaret, I was wrong about the trousers. I shouldn't have let my sister's comments make a difference in the way we conduct our lives. When she and my mother were visiting, I wanted them to approve of what I'd done, the life I'd made with your mother, and Elizabeth's outburst reminded me so much of our father and all that I'd wanted to leave behind. Not the people, if that makes sense, because I did and continue to love them, but their attitudes. And then I behaved just as they wanted me to, I don't know why. I suppose old habits are hard to break. Anyway, girl, you're seventeen now, a young woman, and it's time you stood up for yourself. I'll give you some money and you can buy yourself comfortable clothes for riding. Fair enough?"

Margaret hugged her father and then the mare. The wrangler returned and William bargained a little to bring the asking price down, then the two men walked to the Inland Club to seal the deal with a gentleman's whiskey. Margaret went shopping.

There were so many establishments in Kamloops that Margaret spent a good part of the morning window-shopping. In a druggist's window, a mannequin held a package of headache powders in one hand while the other hand was raised to her forehead as though to massage the pain away. A little pyramid of the powders sat conveniently on a table to her right, should she need more. Passing a bakery, Margaret's mouth watered at the sight of the new loaves arranged in baskets in the window. There was also a shop with photographs in its window, and she stood there for some minutes, looking deep into the images displayed against a background of painted cloth. A wedding party, solemn faces staring out, all except the bride, who was smiling a secret smile, her pale shoulder touching the dark shoulder of her new husband. Various groupings of men in formal suits being handed keys or certificates. One she found almost unbearably sad, the Chinese camp, located a distance from the main part of Kamloops. Margaret guessed that most of the residents were railway workers, but she was shocked at the rows of tents shown in the photograph, the crouched figures in their muddy clothing, one of them looking at the camera with desolate eyes, even some children to one side, up to their ankles in mud. The photograph captured lives lived in squalor and despair, all the more poignant for its placement among the weddings and civil ceremonies of Kamloops. She looked at it for some time, wondering why she felt the way she did. She hadn't known that photographs could do more than provide a picture, but this one seemed to speak a language whose vocabulary she could almost understand.

Margaret found the store she wanted at last, John T. Beaton, Clothier. A sales clerk, dressed in a lovely dress of plaid taffeta with a velvet ribbon tied at her throat, helped Margaret find riding pants of soft green whipcord and a printed broadcloth shirt to go with them. Margaret inhaled the crisp scent of sizing or starch as the clerk led her to a room where she could try them on.

"You look dashing," the clerk told her as she came out of the room in the outfit. "Not many women have been buying trousers, but that will change. There's a lady photographer in town who wears them all the time, and I think she looks wonderful, but some people look at her as though she's committing a terrible sin. Do you need anything else?"

Margaret changed back into her shirtwaist and paid for the clothing, waiting as the clerk wrapped her purchases in brown paper and tied the parcel with string she cut from a huge roll suspended from the ceiling. She wondered if she'd be able to find her way back to the hotel, but with directions from the sales clerk, she was soon walking up to the entrance. Her mother and sisters and brother were sitting outside on chairs set under the trees, the children drinking sarsaparilla from tall glasses beaded with moisture. Jenny ordered one for Margaret, too.

"Father bought the horse, Mother, and he wants me to ride her part of the way home. She's lovely, quite the nicest mare I've seen in a long time, as nice as Daisy in temperament. And you'll never guess! He gave me money to buy proper trousers for riding."

Jenny smiled. "So he's come to his senses about that, has he? I hoped he would."

They sat in the dappled shade for a time, talking quietly of what they'd seen on the streets of Kamloops. Then Jenny took the children up to their rooms to help them get ready for the midday meal, which they ate in the pleasant dining room, joined by William.

"What would you like to do after dinner, Tom? Shall I take you down to the river to watch the sternwheelers?"

"Oh, yes, Father!" cried Tom, and then Jane and Mary asked if they could come, too.

"Certainly," replied William, in an affable mood because of his new horse. "We'll give your mother and sister a break from your chattering."

He took the children to the river, Mary and Jane each holding one of his hands and Tom racing ahead. Jenny and Margaret decided to shop for dress lengths and some notions needed for sewing, and the two walked out to the store Jenny was accustomed to dealing with.

On an autumn trip to the Nicola Valley to celebrate a wedding anniversary, my husband and I stay in the Quilchena Hotel in a room facing the golf course beyond a row of Lombardy poplars. High ceilings and a tall window make the small room feel airy and light. Because I want to know how it feels to ride a horse to the tree line, urge it to a gallop along the ridge I can see from my window, look back to the lake in its bowl of afternoon light, we arrange to rent horses for a few hours.

I have dreamed of a girl, have seen her shadow among the pines.

My husband rides Chief, a tall pinto gelding with the narrow chest of a thoroughbred, and I am given Brownie, a quarter-horse mare with a brand on her left shoulder and a sleek bay coat. While the wrangler is saddling her, I untangle a length of wild rose stem from her mane and smell alfalfa on her breath. Riding her is both familiar and exotic, my muscles remembering the shape of a horse's body but aching in the memory. Crossing Quilchena Creek, her feet toss up little sprays of cold water, but she doesn't stop to drink. Her eyes are fixed on the trail and the rump of the wrangler's horse, Minnie. Along the side of the hill, working to the top, pausing to look out at the perfectly clear sky and the patchwork of hayfield and pasture, green and gold, gold and green, threaded by tawny dirt roads on the valley bottom. Southernwood and dust are in the air, and I can hear magpies and crows squabbling down by the barn when a breeze carries their argument up. A girl riding this slope would have heard the crows, smiled at their quarrel. Her horse's feet would have turned up dust and tiny seeds, her heart might have strained as mine does with longing. My horse is willing to jog, eases into a gallop at the tree line to take me across the ridge until I'm breathless with the beauty of the air and sky. At this high point we see piles of bear scat flecked with rose hips, and there are tall firs dangling cones and aspens on the edge of turning. A hawk hangs in the sky below us.

I have so many questions and no one to ask. How bears can sustain themselves on roses, how wind can make such a subtle perfume of dust and leaves, how a young girl can age in the blink of an eye and never understand, until she is a middle-aged woman in red boots riding a borrowed horse, that something irreplaceable is lost and no one else recognizes the loss. A girl to shadow the woman, to take her hands as they walk into brilliant sunlight or under stars, to sleep beside in darkness, her back unbearably tender in her delicate nightdress. Or to dance with, alone in the grassy field, seeds caught in a strand of hair, the hem of a dress. I swing that girl by the hands, letting her fly out with her long skirt floating in wind. I don't know I've let her go until it's too late to bring her safe into my arms and she is flung into memory.

Eating dinner in the restaurant that evening, I watched from the window, hoping to see her return down the golden hill, swim up from the depths of Nicola Lake, float from the sky in the arms of the wind. No one came, though the little bats swooped under the generous eaves and geese settled in the rushes for the night.

The suite of rooms at the Grand Pacific hummed with excitement as the Stuart family dressed for the concert that evening at the Opera House. Margaret had taken her rose muslin gown out of its case when she'd arrived the night before, and its creases had been eased out with the help of a hotel chambermaid. A simple dress, it suited her dark colouring, and the single strand of milky pearls she wore at her throat was a comely touch. Jenny wore her one formal gown of grey taffeta, sewn from a length brought from Astoria by Aunt Elizabeth, with a cameo on the high collar, a gift from William's mother. She had coiled her long braid into a coronet around her head and fixed it with tortoise-shell combs.

"You will be the loveliest ladies at the concert," William told them, admiring the two as they finished dressing.

"What about us, Father?" Jane and Mary had been ready for some time, having bathed upon their return from the river. Each of them wore a dress of fine white organdy, Mary's gathered at the waist with a blue sash and Jane's with a pale pink sash dotted with rosebuds. Margaret had brushed out their hair from their customary braids and held it back from their foreheads with bands of velvet ribbon she had purchased with her mother that afternoon.

"You look like wild flowers on the slope of Hamilton Mountain, fresh and sweet," he assured them.

Tom wore a suit given him by a Nicola Lake family whose son had outgrown it, and he fidgeted and pulled at the tie which William had helped him to knot. Since returning with his father from the river, where he'd seen the SS *Peerless* beached on the bank, he'd been dreaming of the sternwheelers. William had explained to him that the boats were long past their heyday, the railways had taken over the work of carrying cargo and passengers from one community to another from Shuswap to Savona, and now the sternwheelers were mostly used to move logs. But Tom loved the look of the boats and imagined himself as captain of the *Peerless*, venturing down the Thompson River, as Captain

Irving had, taking flour to the Canadian Pacific Railway crew at Spences Bridge. He was allowed to climb on the *Peerless* in Riverside Park, and his father had paid a man to take Tom's photograph, posed on the portside deck like a sailor.

It wasn't far from the Grand Pacific to the Opera House, just one block south on Fourth Avenue and then west on Victoria Street for slightly more than two blocks. But William had arranged for them to go by carriage so they could arrive in style. Margaret was speechless with excitement as the carriage proceeded along the wide road, past the Fire Hall, the Federal Building, the Bank of Commerce with its ornate stone window headers and rosy brickwork, until they arrived at the Opera House. The driver had to wait his turn to pull up in front of the building, there were so many conveyances delivering concert-goers.

Entering the building and ascending the stairs, Margaret could hardly breathe at the sight of the electric lights, the luxurious wall coverings, and the beautifully dressed people waiting to be shown to their seats. Such gowns and jewels! Margaret had not supposed the women of Kamloops she had seen on her explorations that morning would possess such finery. She felt humbled in her simple muslin dress, but then she remembered how excited she'd been when Father had told the family of the concert and resolved to enjoy every moment of the evening.

William helped them to their seats with the assistance of an usher and then excused himself to return to the lobby to speak to several acquaintances he'd nodded to as they'd entered. Returning just before curtain time, he held a brief whispered conference with his wife and then leaned across Mary and Jane to Margaret.

"Would you like to be presented to Madame Albani later this evening? An old acquaintance, William Slavin, invited me to a reception after the concert. Your mother feels the children should return to the hotel, and she doesn't want to come herself, but she suggested that you might like to accompany me. We wouldn't stay late, and God knows you have so little of this sort of thing that you might like the opportunity."

"Father, how wonderful!"

So it was with doubled excitement that Margaret waited for the curtain to rise upon Madame Albani. The concert was everything she had dreamed it would be. The adored soprano sang a variety of songs from Tosti's "Goodbye" to the poignant "Crossing the Bar." The haunting lines *Twilight and evening bell, And after that the dark!* sent a delicious shiver through Margaret, reminding her of late April evenings when blackbirds fell silent as the darkness settled down on the little valley of the home ranch. This was like poetry or the language of the Bible, this kind of singing. *And may there be no sadness of farewell, When I embark.* Madame Albani's voice was high and true, and she sang with complete poise. She was stunning to look at in her formal gown, her eyes dark and heavy-lidded, her pale throat covered with necklaces. A young singer, the contralto Eva Gauthier, was only able to sing two songs because of the effects of a bad cold, but Margaret marvelled that someone so young could be so accomplished. She sang one duet with the baritone, the closing number, "A Lover and His Lass," and it was wonderful to see them address one another so artfully. And then the baritone sang a rousing encore, "Land of Hope and Glory," which thrilled Margaret to the bone.

After the applause had died down, William leaned to his daughter to ask if she'd enjoyed the concert, but one look at her enraptured face told him all he needed to know. He led his family out to the waiting carriage and returned to the Grand Pacific. "Wait here for me. I'll help your mother up to our rooms," he told Margaret and left her in the carriage to muse and remember. She wondered when the performers, both the experienced and professional Madame Albani and the younger contralto, knew that they would be singers. Had they always loved to sing and pursued it as an avocation, or had someone overheard them and realized that they had the gift, persuading them then to devote their lives to the art of music? If you had a gift, would you know? Margaret wondered about her own life. Apart from horses and the ranch, there was nothing she knew or did well, as far as she knew. She could train young colts, track coyotes, spot the nests of cranes. But was there something she could do for the rest of her life? Oh, why hadn't she thought of it before? Here she was, seventeen, and with no real idea of how her life would proceed. When her father returned to the carriage, she was deep in thought with her face pressed to the window.

Be calm, I want to tell her. Something will come to you, will take you by your shoulders and shake you with its rightness. It will hone your eyes and give you a shape for your stories. But in her seat by the window, Margaret mourned the ordinariness to which she believed she was doomed.

The Slavins' turreted house on Hill Street was brilliant with light, the sound of music floating down to the street. A tennis court to the east of the house was strung with lights, and many people gathered there in the mild evening air, laughing and talking. William introduced his daughter to Mr. and Mrs. Slavin, and Mrs. Slavin led her to the receiving line and waited with her until it was her turn to be presented to Madame Albani.

The great lady was kind and held her hand as she asked her if she lived in Kamloops. She had a way of smiling deep into your eyes and making you feel as though you were the only person in the room, thought Margaret.

"No, we've come from our ranch in the Nicola Valley just to hear you sing," Margaret told her.

"The Nicola Valley! What a lovely name. And you must be the wild rose of the valley. That colour suits you admirably, my dear."

Margaret felt her cheeks go warm. "I loved the Tosti piece that you sang," she told Madame Albani. And 'Crossing the Bar.' It was all so beautiful."

"I'm delighted you enjoyed it. This is my farewell tour of Canada, you know, and when we've completed it, I shall sail to England again where I always feel so much at home. But it is very moving to have been able to sing in such diverse places as your Kamloops and Vienna, one of my favourite cities."

"A farewell tour? Is that why all the songs, or the ones in English anyway, were all about leaving? *And may there be no sadness of farewell, When I embark.* And ending with 'Land of Hope and Glory,' as though to point to your new home?"

"Indeed! And what a clever young lady you are to notice. Your Nicola Valley has taught you to be perceptive. Incidentally, Tosti, who wrote 'Goodbye,' a song I love to sing, is the singing teacher for the Royal Family, and I shall no doubt encounter him in my new life in London. I shall tell him you liked his song, shall I?"

After a few more words, Margaret took her leave, and Mrs. Slavin returned her to her father. He smiled at her.

"Did she speak as beautifully as she sang?"

"Father, to think that such people exist! To be able to sing as she does and to think of something kind to say to girls like me. This is her farewell tour of Canada, she told me, and we won't hear her sing here again."

William took a glass of champagne from a tray offered by a maidservant and put it carefully into Margaret's hand. "Only one, mind you, but the evening seems to warrant it. I wonder if the ranch will be able to hold you now that you've met the Great Canadian Songstress."

Dawn saw the Stuart family settling themselves into the Nicola-Forksdale stage and Margaret mounting the new mare to ride alongside. The mare was well trained but skittish, dancing around as Margaret tried to adjust her stirrups. To get accustomed to the horse and settle her down, the girl decided to ride around the block. South on Fourth, west on Victoria, not a soul to be seen, only a few birds in the small trees newly planted at the edges of the streets. Looking west towards the Opera House, she wondered if last night had been a dream. There was no sign that anything unusual had happened on the quiet thoroughfare. The buildings cast shadows that divided the breadth of street into bars of light and dark, some of the carriage tracks across the smooth dirt in darkness, some in early morning light. Which track had been made by the carriage that had taken her family to such an enchanted evening? And could it really have happened here, in this western town, the golden hills visible even now in the distance?

And no memory in her heart of yearnings for a life different from this one, on a spring street in a western town, the little trees pulsing with their green expectations. Shuttered windows were silent in the morning light. Returning to the waiting stage, Margaret told her father she felt confident enough to set out, the mare having settled. The long road home to the ranch was waiting.

At times on the ride to Trapp Lake, Margaret gave the mare her head and let her gallop along the soft dirt road. The horse was sound-winded, and they made good time. Margaret stopped a few times, once to let the mare drink at a roadside slough and once to stretch her legs while the horse nibbled on a clump of sainfoin in bloom on the edge of a pasture. Sometimes they were ahead of the stage, sometimes behind it, but the day was fine, and when they finally reached the stopping house at Trapp Lake, Margaret felt she could go on until home. Her father wanted to stay with the original plan, however, and rest the mare overnight. After a meal and some conversation about the Miner trial — the police bringing the prisoners to Kamloops had broken the journey at Trapp Lake, and the family who ran the stopping house had stories to tell of the three men sitting on the backboard with blankets around their shoulders in the pouring rain — the stage proceeded towards Forksdale and August Jackson, who awaited the family's return at the Douglas Lake road.

In such ways is the world remembered. A box of slatted wood containing photographs, letters, the program from a concert in an unlikely place, as unlikely as David Daniels singing "*Ombra mai fu*" in a hall on a remote bus line. Driving through Kamloops nine decades later, I try to see the streets as she would have seen them, at dawn, riding the new bay mare. Although some of the houses remain, the vistas — the river, the golden hills rising from the town's western reach — are flattened somehow, and the sound is traffic, shrill machinery, not the soft burr of voices as people walk to work in the shadow of sleeping buildings or harness horses in the stableyards. No young woman in plaid taffeta glides through the quiet streets to her job at John T. Beatton, Clothier, where she would spend the morning folding petticoats of fine lawn and dream of the young assistant at the Bank of British Columbia; instead, a girl in tattered jeans with a golden ring through her lip, sipping from a paper cup, headphones clinging to her ears. I listen for the sound of the printing presses issuing news of the bank robbers and reviews of a concert in the Opera House and hear only a motorcycle accelerating as a light turns green. And dust, yes, descendent certainly from the dust that settled as Margaret rode, as the stars shed their outer skins and windowsills flaked in the weather.

Chapter Six

SOMEONE HAS BROUGHT IN a sampler, asking if I thought it was artistic enough for my exhibition. The lender, a small woman in her eighties, told me it had been stitched by her sister on a visit from her home in Ireland. It was surrounded with a gilt frame and arrived wrapped in several layers of tea towels, themselves worthy of display for their fabric — fine linen which the woman told me had come from Belfast in the year of her marriage to a local fisherman. She'd received a bolt of it, and it had lasted her until now; she simply cut a length of it as she needed new towels and then hemmed and ornamented them in some way, perfect edgings of cross-stitches or nosegays of flowers and a homily, *Thou crownest the year with thy goodness*, framed with a wreath of silvery willow leaves. The sampler itself was pleasant, a little harbour of fishing boats of the sort common in the thirties and forties, blue sea, trees on the shore, and a verse from John Masefield:

> *I must go down to the seas again, to the lonely sea*
> *and the sky,*
> *And all I ask is a tall ship and a star to steer her by.*

I assured her that the sampler was indeed artistic enough, but that I would also love to use her tea towels. She was quite skeptical about any museum that might want to display tea towels, but I explained my idea that history is contained in the small details, the homely objects, and by putting together a lot of them, we might be able to understand something about a community in a particular time and place.

"If you only saw armour or cannons, then those are the only activities you would think mattered. But what about the way people, maybe ordinary people, spent their days? Did they farm or cook or sew? Of course they did. I want to concentrate on textiles and fabrics because for so long they were the way that women explored their creativity, often unconsciously. These tea towels are such a wonderful example! If you were just thinking of them as purely practical, as cloths to wipe the dishes with, you probably wouldn't have taken such care to make them pretty."

"Aye," she replied in her soft voice, a faint Irish brogue still discernable. "I used to look through my Bible for a verse that suited how I was feeling and then try to match it with flowers or some such. Well, if you're serious about the tea towels, Anna, I can bring you lots of them."

I told her I was very serious. We had a cup of tea together, and she told me that her father had worked in the linen mills as a weaver. He was very proud of the linen he wove and used to say that its softness came from the water of the creek harnessed for the washing and bleaching process. Soft northern Irish water and then line-drying in the soft air. The bolt of linen had come from her parents as a wedding gift after she'd left Ireland to come to Canada and this community as a young school teacher, met a local fisherman and decided to make her home with him. I told her I'd like to include a little of her story on a card which would be displayed with her tea towels and sampler, and she seemed very pleased. She left, assuring me that she would return with more of her fancy-work.

I spend some time photographing the items I'll be using for the exhibit in order to archive them properly. Each object will be accompanied by a full description. But what it won't say, could never say, is how the fabrics came to their softness, decades of carefully drying teacups and plates, the weight of sleeping lovers, the endless washing and hanging out in sunlight and fog, smoothing and folding, pressing with hot irons until they gave up their wrinkles and entered dark cupboards to wait, scented with lavender and the faint memory of wind.

And then I look at some of the photographs in Margaret's box, trying to name each person from the references in the letters. Her grandmother, younger sisters and brother, only one of a couple that might be her parents, a young man hanging photographs on a line with clothes pegs as though they were the clothing of infants. And what photographs are they, hanging in the air like the shadows of shadows, souls on their way to the country in the west?

"What will we name her?" William asked, watching the new mare roll in the dust in the home corral. She had closed her eyes and was luxuriating in the dry dust, lingering for a moment to rub one shoulder, then the other. It had been her first night at Cottonwood, and Margaret had awoken several times to look out to make sure she was still there, not spirited away by the darkness. In the moonlight, the mare had been alert, listening to the other horses, nickering to them in return. After she grew accustomed to her new surroundings, she would be pastured with the saddle horses the family kept at the home ranch.

Margaret had already decided on a name. Riding the mare on the road south of Kamloops, she'd noticed again how the black forelock resembled a thistle. And when she'd stopped to let the mare crop at a rich patch of pink-blossoming sainfoin, she'd seen the horse nip off the tip of a blossoming thistle, a few mauve petals falling away as she chewed.

"I've already named her Thistle, Father. Do you think it suits her?"

"Well, now, I suppose I'd hoped for something more stately,

to suit her role as our top brood mare. But Thistle, yes, it does suit her with that forelock. Thistle she is, then."

According to records given them by the mare's previous owner, they could expect a heat in the next few weeks. The plan was to breed Thistle to the ranch's stud and begin to develop a quarter horse ideally suited to the Cottonwood's range. Thistle's broad chest and sound wind, the strong legs of the Bonny Prince — a legacy of his Clydesdale ancestors — and the cutting ability and endurance that came with both horses: William imagined generations of foals with this combination bringing in the cattle each fall and driving them high up the plateau each spring. Generation upon generation, the bay mare, the dark stallion, the dry air alive with their descendants in the fields of the valley and mountain.

"May I ride her to Spahomin tomorrow, Father? I'd like to spend a day or two with Grandmother Jackson and tell her about the concert. I've already made sure Mother doesn't need me."

"Certainly you may, but don't forget we've planned to go to the Victoria Day celebrations down at Nicola Lake. So you'll only be able to stay the one night. Ask your grandmother if she'd like to come with us on Thursday. August could bring her as far as the ranch on his way, or else we could meet there if August is taking his family."

"I'll ask, but she usually doesn't like to go to things like that. There's always drinking, and she doesn't approve of Indians taking a drink. She never minds when you drink whiskey, Father, but she hates to see August drink, or anyone else from the Reserve. Why is that?"

"Oh, it's a long story, Margaret. She's seen a lot in her years, both good and bad, and she knows what life was like before the valley was settled by ranchers, although there would have been trappers in her childhood. She's right to mistrust alcohol, it's caused a lot of sorrow to her people."

The next day saw Margaret riding towards Douglas Lake along the Nicola River. The sunflowers were in their prime, full and brilliant yellow, there were clusters of long-leaved phlox, and threaded through the willows on the riverbank, the buds of white clematis were just opening. Margaret loved clematis. For the next month, there'd be heavenly white clouds of it all along the river and the creek running through the home ranch, and then, until winter, fluffy seedheads would cling to the vines, some of them floating away on the wind to plant themselves in any cranny. Higher up, on the summer range, she'd found blue clematis and had tried bringing a root of it home to try by the veranda, but it had withered and died, longing for the high air of the mountains, or that was what she liked to imagine.

Fresh bear scat by the river spooked Thistle a little, and Margaret found it difficult to keep her down to a walk or a quick nervous trot. Yet she was not familiar enough with the mare's habits to let her run. This was unfamiliar country to a horse raised on the banks of the Thompson River, where the hazards were rattle-snakes and small stinging cacti. It was gone noon by the time they reached the Reserve, and Margaret was glad to find her grandmother's house full of the smell of frying trout.

Embracing her grandmother, she was startled to see a strange man sitting in the chair of woven willow and sinew on the other side of the stove. He leapt to his feet, striding across the room and holding out his hand to take hers in a firm handshake. He had very blue eyes and coppery hair, and he was wearing a pair of Grandmother's moccasins, beaded and quilled.

"You must be Margaret. Your grandmother has been telling me about you. I'm Nicholas Byrne, how do you do?"

Grandmother Jackson handed him a plate of trout and bannock as if it was the most natural thing in the world to have a young man at her stove. She handed Margaret a plate, too. As they sat at the table to eat their lunch, the man explained that he was at Spahomin at the suggestion of James Teit of Spences Bridge.

"I'm translating his book on the Thompson people into French as a graduate project for Dr. Boas at Columbia University. Do you know his work?"

Dr. Boas? The only doctor the two women knew was Dr. Tuthill at Nicola Lake, though William spoke of Dr. Sutton, whom Margaret slightly remembered, and a Dr. Chipp, whom she'd never known at all. Dr. Tuthill's work was mending broken bones, sewing up cuts, doctoring people who were down with influenza, and even tending to the man who was shot at Chapperon Lake. Why would a doctor need Mr. Teit's book translated into French? Margaret said as much to Nicholas Byrne.

"Oh, I'm sorry, that's not the kind of doctor I mean. Dr. Boas is a doctor of anthropology, he studies different cultures. I'm a student of his at Columbia, in New York City. Mr. Teit has been doing some work for Dr. Boas, gathering infor-mation about the Indian people of this area, and people in Europe are very interested. Dr. Boas has been translating it into German — he comes from Germany — and he suggested that I do the same into French. My mother is French, so I've been brought up to speak both English and French."

Margaret knew Mr. Teit. He'd come to the valley before, often, and had spent time with her grandmother, asking her about how she made her baskets and even buying a few for a museum. He was a nice man, and Grandmother spoke highly of him, impressed that he was so interested in not just her baskets but in the stories of her people and her language, which he spoke quite well. Once he'd accompanied her on a plant-gathering trip and had written down the names of the plants she pointed out in the Thompson language, taking notes on what they were used for and how they were prepared. He'd come to the ranch, too, and had several meals with the Stuart family. His own first wife had been an Indian woman, Lucy Antko from Cook's Ferry, and he was trusted by almost everyone.

"Are you staying with my grandmother?" asked Margaret, a little uncomfortable at the prospect of a stranger sleeping in the small cabin.

"No, with your uncle August and his family. But your grandmother has invited me to go for plants with her. I didn't know you'd be visiting, and I don't want to get in the way. Do you mind if I come along?"

"Of course not," Margaret replied, but in fact she was a little shy in the company of this young man. He was unlike the cowhands and ranchers who formed her experience of masculine company. She wondered if she looked as untidy as she felt, her hair windblown. And what was he doing with moccasins on his feet? Her heart was beating a little faster than usual, it seemed, and she wondered if he could tell.

"Have you been at Spahomin long?" she asked.

"I came three days ago, just as all the excitement about capturing of the train robbers had begun to die down. Though I must admit it's thrilling to think of such a dangerous gang at large in one's own back yard, so to speak!"

Margaret was so irritated to hear his version of the story that she forgot she wasn't going to speak about the capture. "You don't know much if you think of them as dangerous. We all knew George Edwards, the man they're saying is really Bill Miner. He lived and worked here for a few years, and he came to all sorts of social events. The dangerous ones, if you ask me, were the police who were shooting at everything that moved when they cornered Mr. Edwards and his friends last week. They were sitting by a campfire, doing nothing more dangerous than making lunch, when the policeman accused them of robbing a mail train."

"You sound as though you were there. Can that be possible?" Mr. Byrne sounded more surprised than shocked.

"I'd rather not talk about it any longer." Margaret got up and poured strong tea into mugs for the three of them and brought a bowl of sugar to the table. Then she went out to the covered box in the shallows of the creek where her grandmother kept the milk. It was foolish to be upset with someone who was a stranger to the country and its happenings, she thought, and anyway it wasn't like her to fly off the handle. He seemed quite nice, and Grandmother obviously liked him enough to feed him and invite him on plant trips. She returned to the kitchen and drank her tea, listening to the young man describe his journey across America by train to Seattle and then his meeting with Mr. Teit at Spences Bridge.

"He is a knowledgeable man, I can see why Dr. Boas likes him so well. He says he takes out hunters who visit from all parts of the continent and he helps to run his father-in-law's orchard at Nine Mile Ranch. He told me all about the irrigation system they have for their trees. I wouldn't have believed apples could produce so abundantly in that dry country, but he says the soil is ideal, they only have to supply the water."

"Yes," Margaret replied. "We trade beef for Spences Bridge apples. My father knows the Smith family, and we get boxes of their apples. And they're wonderful, especially the Grimes Goldens. Mrs. Smith wins prizes for them. Last year she won a silver medal for apples she sent to the Colonial Fruit Show at the Royal Horticultural Society in London, England. It was on the front page of our newspaper. I like to think of her apples travelling across the ocean to win prizes!"

"Mrs. Smith is marvellous. I met the family while I was with Mr. Teit, and I was impressed with Mrs. Smith's dedication to her orchards," Nicholas responded. "It's only a year since her husband died, Mr. Teit told me, and she's determined to carry on his work. The orchards were lovely, too. I think there's no flower more perfect than a branch of apple blossom. My mother has an apple tree that she's coddled along in our garden in New York. It's called Seek-No-Further. I can't imagine a better name for anything. But the trouble is, although it's covered with blossoms each spring, there are only ever a few apples. I don't suppose there's another tree nearby to pollinate it."

They finished their tea and then gathered some of Grandmother's baskets together to take on their hunt for plants. Margaret's favourite was a berry basket of split cedar root with a design of natural red and dyed-black bitter cherry bark. It had two soft deerskin straps so that it could be worn on the back, leaving the hands free for picking. Grandmother had made it as a young woman, excited by all possibilities of design, and had used a complex pattern of deer hoof and entrail. There had been another colour, sun-bleached stems of reed grass, but over the years the basket itself had faded and become soiled from use, and now the grass stems were indistinguishable from the rest of the roots.

"This is very beautiful," said Nicholas, looking at the basket's intricate pattern. He ran a finger along the design to feel the texture of the imbrication.

"My grandmother is really an expert basket-maker," Margaret told him. "The one you're using is a shape she adapted from the fish baskets to be used as a saddlebag. See, it's got a flat side so it can sit against the horse's flank. That design is meant to be summer lightning, something you'll see quite a lot of if you stay around this area for long. And the basket Grandmother is using is a more typical shape, sort of conical."

"Do you make many of them, Mrs. Jackson?"

"I have what I can use for now. Some of the ladies make them to sell to whites, but I don't want to spend so much time on a basket and then not know where it's going. I give a few away — to Margaret's family, of course, and the priest has one, and Mr. Teit bought some for a museum, some that I had and wasn't using, some that were done completely in the old way, one or two even that my mother had made. He told me it was important that they be saved to show how we did things before the whites came."

Nicholas nodded. "I agree with him. I've seen some of the Coast Salish baskets in the Smithsonian Institution, and all sorts of other things, too. So many people have no idea about native cultures, and the museums are one way to educate them. Not the best, I'm afraid. The artifacts always look out of place, somehow, even when they try to give them a context."

They were walking in back of the Reserve towards the small

sloughs that dotted the higher fields. Margaret was looking for nodding onions, which her grandmother liked to use to flavour meat. The bulbs themselves were pretty to look at, pink and elongated, and they tasted delicious. They were eaten fresh, but some were dried for winter, tied into bunches. Soaking the dried bulbs in water for a few minutes made them taste almost fresh in the winter soup pots. They were also looking for the pale mauve lilies which could be found under pines as soon as the snow melted. These were a favourite spring food.

(I want to hold the girl, smooth her hair, tell her that whatever happens, I'm waiting in time to trace the lines of memory caught in a basket of coiled root, fine imbrications of cherry bark and reeds. Her hands with their long fingers, the slight bones of her ankles, the cup of her throat. Thinking of her, my own throat tightens.)

"What kind of grass are we walking on?" Nicholas asked.

"Oh, this is mostly bunchgrass, the best grass for horses and cattle," Margaret told him. "Our cattle feed most of the year on this, all the cattle in the valley do, and they make the best beef. Even the wild game in the valley tastes better than anywhere else because of the air and this forage."

By now Grandmother Jackson had dug up many of the pretty green onion plants, their flowers still furled in the tight green sepals. She was careful not to take too many from any one place, and she shook the dirt from each loosened clump, mindful of the tiny bulblets that were too small to take; these she tucked carefully back into the soil. In a grove of pines they found lots of mariposa lilies, and Margaret explained that they ate many kinds of lilies, but this was usually the first in the spring to be ready, and its season was quite long. Many of the others were dug after they'd flowered, the blue camas and orange tiger, for instance, but these ones were a spring treat, eaten raw or else steamed if you could find enough to take home.

They came to one of the little sloughs and sat on the shore to rest. Bulrushes surrounded the slough, and Margaret pointed out a yellow-headed blackbird nest, fastened to a clump of bulrushes like a tiny basket. "Look, there's the male, see, he's got white patches on his wings. He's nervous because we're here. There must be a red-winged pair nesting around here, too, because you hear them whistling. Do you hear, just there?"

Nicholas looked at her in surprise. "How do you know this?"

"You mean, about the birds?"

"No, I mean all of it! The plants, the baskets, and yes, the birds, too. I hear the sound, of course, but it just sounds like, well, birds." Nicholas smiled. "I guess I've always imagined myself to be an outdoorsman because my family has a summer camp in the Adirondacks, in upstate New York. But I couldn't tell you what birds were there, or plants, for that matter, apart from roses. My mother loves roses and is always pointing out the best features of her moss roses and her bourbons. And I guess I know a bit about insects from fly-fishing, because you have to know what flies are active before you choose your fly to cast."

"Well, that's only how I know anything, really. You've seen that my grandmother knows about plants, and she takes me with her when I come to visit. And I ride with my father as often as I can, when I'm not helping my mother or at school, and he loves birds. Anyway, how could you live here and not notice the blackbird's whistle and want to know what bird makes that sound? It's one of the first signs of spring, especially at home, because a creek runs through our home ranch, and lots of blackbirds nest there. I love to lie in my bed in the morning and hear them calling back and forth to one another. Father says the spring song is all about territory, but I think it sounds joyous, like music."

"I'd like to meet your father. Would that be possible?"

Margaret was suddenly tongue-tied. She tried to imagine this unusual young man in her family home, talking to her father. Would her father like him? And why did it matter? He was looking at her so intently that she swallowed quickly and found her voice.

"I'm sure you'd be welcome at the ranch anytime. Perhaps you'll call on us for Sunday dinner?"

Her grandmother encouraged the young man to talk about his work. They learned he was twenty-two and had completed a university degree the previous year. Although he had intended to read law, as his father had, he had become interested in the anthropology course he'd taken in his second year of studies. Encouraged by Dr. Boas, he pursued a degree in this field and had assisted his mentor in preparing monographs on the Indians of the west coast for the American Museum of Natural History. But it was the monograph written by Mr. Teit that had really captured his attention, and Dr. Boas had suggested that he make the translation to partly fulfill the requirements for a further degree.

That night, over a supper of lily bulbs and more of the sweet fried trout, Margaret told her grandmother about the concert in Kamloops. She tried to describe her feelings as she listened to the unfamiliar music, which spoke to her as clearly as a well-loved person might, spoke of life's changes and deep love of country and home with such yearning and emotion. She spoke of meeting Madame Albani at the Slavin house and of riding Thistle down the deserted morning street with its shadows and phantom carriage tracks telling a strange tale of the evening before. Her grandmother listened, saying little, wondering at this girl, beloved and yet mysterious. She had felt helpless when her own daughter had gone to live with the priest, wearing a severe black dress, but she had not felt that her daughter contained depths she was incapable of knowing. Jenny had been swept up in the tide of Christianity that had been too overwhelming at the time to resist. So much had come with it, been tied to it and lost by it. It took Mrs. Jackson some time to find a way to live her own life comfortably in the face of such alien authority. And she discovered it wasn't the gods or spirits who had changed. They could be found still in their old haunts, in the sky and water, living in the body of an animal, asking nothing more or less than they had always expected. This other god that the priests worshipped and encouraged the Indians to worship — there was no more sign of him than of any other Great Spirit, though the priests said he was all-seeing and all-knowing and could number the hairs on a person's head, such was the greatness of his love. Mrs. Jackson felt this was not of much use to a person and that a god as powerful as the priests said he was ought to have done something worthwhile, like curing the terrible outbreaks of smallpox or other diseases brought by the whites. In the house the priests had built for this god at Douglas Lake, you could look through the high windows during Mass and see hawks or ospreys teaching their young to fish. The shadows of clouds moved across the hills like herds of foraging cattle in the early morning light, and this was something to think on while the priest spoke dramatically in a language the Indians had never heard before.

Since the day that Margaret had arrived with the crane's bone and asked to be told about the ceremonies of the young women, the old woman had treasured the times the girl came to her, eager to learn about plants, about baskets, about her own girlhood before the ranches had filled the valley with fences and cattle. She marvelled at the girl's ability with horses, her boundless energy, her willingness to do any task her grandmother set out for her. A few times they participated in the women's sweat baths, and it was comforting to sit in the small lodge with the girl beside her, waiting for the heated rocks to be brought in. On the floor, fresh fir boughs and juniper they had cut earlier in the day. Margaret had almost fainted the first time, squatting with the three other women in the intense heat, but her grandmother held her arm and helped her to breathe deeply. After, they had plunged into the creek and scrubbed themselves with branches of fir. The old woman's sadness at her own daughter's early departure to the priests was soothed by her daughter's child.

Lying in bed that night, Margaret heard Thistle stirring outside the window. The horse, tethered to a fence, whickered nervously as coyotes called to one another in the far hills. Margaret got up and looked out. There was a high three-quarter moon, and the yard was silver with its light. She felt excited, although she wasn't sure why. Watching her horse in the starry yard, she felt an urge to go out quickly and ride in the moonlight. Making sure her grandmother was asleep, she quietly left the cabin, wearing only her light cotton nightdress. Approaching Thistle, she spoke to the horse softly, so as not to startle her. She untethered her, vaulting onto the mare's back, and using her hand on Thistle's neck to guide her, she directed her to the trail leading up behind the cabin to the moon-burnished hill. What was this feeling of wanting to enter the night? And how could you, in your mortal form? To disappear into blackness, the place where you stood in the dust untouched by your footsteps, hearing the coyote's cry as a part of yourself, a thrilling cry from your heart's own centre, wanting to share the riddle of this darkness, punctuated by stars, Oh, but with whom? Thistle was reluctant to leave the safety of the trail, and Margaret could feel her tremble when the coyotes yipped, a little nearer by now, so she turned back on the trail and returned to the yard.

From the window of his room in August Jackson's cabin, Nicholas Byrne, also sleepless, was startled to see a horse coming down the hill, and on its back a girl dressed in starlight. He wondered if he was dreaming until the girl slid off the horse and he realized it was Margaret Stuart. She was wearing a nightdress, he could see, and he could also see the shape of her body through the thin fabric. Apart from paintings and the sculptures in the New York museums, he'd never seen a girl dressed in so little. The sight was otherworldly, the horse with its nostrils flaring, the girl, nearly naked, stroking its dark neck under those extraordinary stars. What a place this was, he thought, and returned to his bed, eager for the morning.

At the fete at Nicola Lake on Victoria Day, Margaret participated in the Ladies' Race and came second. After the ribbons were presented, she came to her family with her eyes shining and her cheeks flushed, the rosette of blue satin pinned to her blouse. She'd loved the excitement of running in the warm May air, past the crowds of cheering spectators, her legs feeling powerful and strong as she raced for the finish line. She wished they had thought to bring a saddle horse so she could enter the Hurdles; the team that drew their buggy were broken to saddle, but they certainly weren't jumpers.

"I feel so lucky I could even win the Cowboy Race," she announced. In previous years, she had stood with her mother, watching everything but not willing to run or ride in the gymkhana events, always uncertain whether to enter the regular races or the Indian ones. The Quarter Mile Pony, for which the prizes were a cup for first and ten dollars for second place, or the half-mile dash, Klootchman, which rewarded the winner with ten dollars, and five for the one who came second. She wondered if she'd be challenged if she tried to enter the wrong race or simply steered to the one the organizers thought appropriate. This year, after her race, she was happy to take her sisters to greet families they knew, to picnic under a Lombardy poplar on a clean white cloth, to gather with others to watch the Nicola Polo Club, with her father on a horse brought for him from a neighbouring ranch, beat the Quilchena Club handily. The cyclists came in, one by one, from the Challenge Cup race, and the winner drank from the silver cup in great, thirsty gulps. It was a wonderful day, from the parade in the morning, which the Stuarts had watched from the porch of Tom Carrington's store, to the drive home under stars with the horses trotting alertly along the moonlit road while bats flitted under cottonwoods and coyotes yipped beyond the shoulder of hill rising from the road.

Three days after Victoria Day, Nicholas headed to the Cotton-wood Ranch with one of August's children, who had agreed to ride halfway with him and direct him. He was becoming accustomed to the western style of riding, with a longer stirrup, the saddle with its high horn and cantle, the way one had to hold the reins in one hand and direct the horse by pressing them against the animal's neck. It was certainly beautiful country to ride in, and he knew now why people spoke of a big sky. He'd never seen anything like it, apart from his views of the American plains from the train, and he marvelled at the way it went on forever in every direction. You could feel your head clear as you rode under it. He also understood now why one of his Columbia classmates had often spoken longingly of the open spaces of his home state, Montana. This must have been how Peter felt, riding on his home ranch near Helena, as though anything was possible under such a sky. There was no sense of constriction, of a vista cut off by mountains or buildings. He could see mountains, yes, but beyond them as well. His feeling that he was riding on the spine of the earth was part of his intense elation as he rode toward the Cottonwood Ranch, saying farewell to Davey with the ranch in sight in the distance.

Margaret was helping her mother with the dinner preparations. Her father had been curious about Nicholas Byrne, having heard about him from other ranchers and from August, who had come over for advice on a horse a day or two after the Stuarts had returned from Kamloops. August's impression had been favour-able, and he'd told William that the young man had tried to buy a pair of Mrs. Jackson's moccasins to wear because he said they made his feet feel as though they'd come home. She had smiled and refused his money, saying he was welcome to the shoes as long as he wore them with respect. William had tried to question Margaret about Nicholas, but she only blushed and said he'd see for himself. That told him something he wasn't sure he wanted to know, though seeing her at the Slavin house on the night of the concert in Kamloops told him something was developing he wasn't quite prepared for. He was so accustomed to her company, so convinced of her good sense and judgment, that he hadn't much thought of her as young or old, just Margaret. But seeing her in that rose dress with the little string of pearls around her throat, he realized that she'd become a lovely young woman. One day a child on a pony, long braids flying behind her, the next, well, this beauty. And if he noticed, he felt certain others would as well.

When Nicholas Byrne came riding down the dirt lane into the ranch yard, announced by the dogs, Margaret was waiting on the porch; she had seen the puffs of dust from the horse's hooves on the dry lane before she saw anything else. William came out of the barn, introduced himself, and led Nicholas's horse away to be unsaddled and turned out in a corral. And then Margaret greeted the young man and offered him a seat on the porch, but he told her he'd rather see the ranch buildings, if that was possible.

"I'll just introduce you to my mother and ask if she needs me for anything before dinner."

The kitchen was at the back of the house, and Margaret wondered what Nicholas's impression was as she led him through the front room — no parlour here, just a comfortable room with big armchairs and lots of books on pine shelves made from trees on their own land, trees that William had cut and planed for the house he had built in the fourth year of his marriage. A table with a chess set on top, anticipating the next move, against a wall under a low window looking out on the garden. A hearth of stones selected from the Nicola River. A battered violin case on the floor, a needlepoint frame with the beginnings of a sampler. Some of Grandmother Jackson's baskets on shelves, one on the hearth holding kindling. She wondered if his home in New York was anything like the Slavin house in Kamloops, which was now her idea of how people in cities and towns must live. The kitchen was fragrant with roasting meat and a pie made from the last of the dried apples. Cream from the Jersey cow had been whipped and sweetened and sat waiting on the deep windowsill. Jenny Stuart wiped her hands on her apron and stepped forward to shake Nicholas's outstretched hand and welcome him to the ranch.

"It's very nice of you to let me come for dinner," he responded. "Your mother has been so good to me, too, and your brother, taking pity on me when they saw my tent and offering me a bed, making meals for me. I hadn't expected to be treated so well, being a stranger to you all."

"Strangers are welcome here," Jenny replied in her low voice. "We just don't have the opportunity to meet many or to give them dinner." She smiled at Nicholas and turned to the work table, where she was chopping the first scallions from the garden to brighten the mashed potatoes and turnips.

Margaret and Nicholas went out to the barn, where William was watering the Bonny Prince and putting fresh straw in his box stall. The stallion came to the half-door of his stall and allowed them to pat his neck and admire him. Then they walked up the spacious middle aisle of the barn, William explaining about the bawling cow in one stall, a lame horse in another. Nicholas's horse loudly rattled his bucket of oats. The smell of dry hay was sweet, and the midday sunlight shone in shafts through the open door and windows, illuminating the dust motes that hung in the air like gilded insects. Barn swallows were building their nests on the high beams, flying in from the creek with pellets of mud, plucking straw from the unused stalls. One flew back and forth from the coyote skull over the harness room door, tucking mud and straw into the fractured cheek. The two men and the girl walked out into the yard, a few horses in the home corrals watching with mild curiosity, Daisy coming to the fence when she saw Margaret with the men. Nicholas asked about the growing season, the weather, the beef market. "We take our cattle to Kamloops now, it used to be Fort Hope, over the Coquihalla Pass, and that was a journey, I tell you, having done it myself the first year I had cattle to ship. But soon there'll be a rail line all the way to Nicola Lake from Spences Bridge, they hope to extend it as far as Coutlee by this summer, Nicola itself by next spring. We'll be able to ship the cattle much more efficiently, not so much weight loss and loss of condition as there is now." When the dinner bell rang, the two men were talking easily together, and Margaret ran ahead to wash and to make sure the table was ready.

When they all took their places, Jane and Mary seated on either side of Nicholas, Margaret thought how nice the room looked in the May light. The best tablecloth dressed the table, a white damask edged with Honiton lace, a gift from Aunt Elizabeth one Christmas. There was a fine rib roast, bowls of the last of the winter vegetables mashed with butter and flecked with spring onion, cut glass dishes of serviceberry relish and green tomato pickle, a little pot of shredded horseradish mellowed with thick cream, and jugs of icy spring water and fresh milk. A basket of coiled cedar root was filled with biscuits covered with a linen cloth. In the middle of the table, a blue willow vase held the first sweet peas of the year from the vines trained on netting against the eastern wall of the house.

"Ah, this looks good, Jenny, my love." William stood at the end of the table, carving thick slices of beef, the ones close to the middle of the joint nicely pink in their centres. Margaret took the platter of meat around the table, helping each person to the slice he or she chose. Her mother served vegetables and gravy, and Jane took the bowls of condiments to those who asked for them. William said a brief grace, and everyone began to eat. For the first part of the meal there was little conversation. But as first servings disappeared and those wanting seconds were helped to meat or vegetables or another high golden biscuit, William began to ask Nicholas about his work.

"Well, I understand that you know Mr. Teit, sir. You know then, of course, that he has published several monographs on the Indian people here in the Nicola Valley as well as on the tribes at Lillooet and some others. I've been studying under Dr. Franz

Boas at Columbia University, and he is a great admirer of Mr. Teit's work. In fact, he commissioned much of the research that Mr. Teit has undertaken. I'm working on my master's degree, and Dr. Boas suggested that I should translate the monograph on the Thompson Indians into French, because there is great interest in this material in Europe. I began the work this winter, and I was enchanted, I suppose you could say, by the descriptions of the Thompson people and their lives. I wanted to see it all for myself though I know that much of what Teit describes — the religious ceremonies and the hunting and fishing rituals, for instance — is no longer the usual practise. And I've been trying to visit each village, from the small ones below Lytton to Slaz, near the Cornwall ranch, to Quilchena, which I gather is the last real Thompson village before the Okanagans begin. Though Mr. Teit told me that Spahomin is as much Thompson as Okanagan, and I've been hearing both languages about equally. He felt I should meet Mrs. Stuart's mother to see the finest baskets around and to talk to her about her knowledge of medicines and plants."

"You are certainly right to do that. Jenny's mother, of all the elders at Spahomin, has an amazing memory, and, more than that, she continues many of the traditional ways and knows why they're important."

"Yes, she's a wonderful woman. I've been talking to her about baskets, and she's given me a wealth of information. She even has me making a little coiled basket though I'm all thumbs. But she says the only way to really know is to do. So I'm doing, or trying at least!"

Margaret smiled. When her grandmother had begun to teach her to make baskets, she, too, had five thumbs on each hand. She cried when the split root refused to coil evenly, and her first imbrications were untidy and irregular. Now she could make a passable basket, but nothing like what her grandmother could do with her eyes closed. And often it seemed as if that was how she was making them, because she could coil perfectly without even looking at the emerging basket on her lap, her hands and fingers working as though of their own accord. Fly patterns, arrows, nets . . . she would reach for strands of bitter cherry, pale grasses, and the design would emerge from the surface of the basket.

After dinner, Margaret cleared the table and drew a jug of hot water from the reservoir on the stove to add to the cold water she had pumped into the sink. She began to wash the dishes and was startled to hear Nicholas ask where he might find a tea towel to begin the drying.

"Oh, you don't have to help. You're a guest! Why don't you sit on the porch in the shade?"

"I'd like to help," he answered. "I'm perfectly capable of drying dishes, and it's nice to be in this kitchen. Anyway, I have a motive. If I help, you'll be finished that much quicker, and I'd hoped you could ride part way back with me. I noticed some unusual pink flowers, well, maybe they're very ordinary, but I've never seen them before. Anyway, they're blooming by the road about a mile from here, and I know you'll be able to tell me what they are."

He stacked the dried dishes on the worktable, and Margaret put them away after she'd finished washing the pots and scalding the dishcloth. She could smell him there by the sink, a nice smell, like her father after a bath — some sort of soap, and damp hair. When his arm brushed hers, a thin flame of lightning ran up her spine and spread out along her shoulder blades. When she tried to speak after that, her words were thick in her mouth. She wondered if he could tell. Did she want to accompany him part way home? She nodded a wordless yes.

(Whatever happens, I am waiting. The cup of her throat, her small breasts . . .)

111

THERESA KISHKAN

Margaret's parents were agreeable to her escorting Nicholas part of the way back to Spahomin, and so, after making arrangements for the young man to return to spend a day or two in the high country in the next week, they said their goodbyes. Nicholas and Margaret, who had changed into her riding pants, went out to saddle the horses. Margaret decided to take Daisy, who had not been ridden since Thistle had been brought home to the ranch; she brought out her saddle, struggling with the cinch as Daisy moved about as far as her rope would allow her. Nicholas's borrowed horse, a dun gelding, waited patiently while Margaret settled Daisy, who pranced and sidestepped excitedly. Then they rode out to the road and headed toward Douglas Lake.

"Look at that thunderhead! We often get storms after a hot day. They don't last long, an hour or two at the most, but the sky is spectacular, even so."

Nicholas looked to where Margaret pointed. A huge cloud formation filled the southwestern sky, lit from behind by the falling sun. They rode on, letting the horses lope a bit and reining them in by a low-growing clump of pink flowers.

"There! That's the plant I meant. It looks almost like a cactus or succulent with its fat leaves."

Margaret got off her horse and Nicholas followed. She bent to the clump of flowers and dug around with her fingers underneath. Pulling up a few white stringy bits of root, she said, "This is bitterroot, it's one of the most important food plants of my grandmother's people. They would dig big sacks of this in spring, earlier than now actually, this clump is a bit late. They'd peel the roots and dry them, and they'd use them all winter. Grandmother Jackson told me that bitterroot would be traded for dried salmon with the people over on the Fraser River and the lower Thompson. It was very good for you, although I thought the pudding my grandmother made so I could taste it was awfully bitter. No one had much sugar, so they'd use dried berries, I guess."

"The flowers are lovely. I thought of you when I saw them."

Margaret blushed, looking at the soft pink blooms. She got back on her horse and rode a little further, followed by Nicholas. By now, the thunderclouds were almost directly overhead and big drops of rain began to fall.

"We should get out of the open right away, because this storm is too close. See that stand of cottonwoods over there? We'll head for that. It's safer to wait it out under a group of trees than to stay in the open or near just one tree."

As they reached the trees, a clap of thunder startled the horses. Margaret dismounted and pulled a rope out of her saddlebag, hobbling Daisy deftly. Nicholas watched as she did the same with his horse. Each time thunder rumbled around them, the horses would snort and lay back their ears, the whites of their eyes showing. But both showed the good sense to stay in the sheltered area, and anyway, hobbled, they couldn't have run.

"Did I embarrass you with my comment about the flower? I'm sorry, but I got carried away. Your skin is so lovely, particularly when you blush."

"No one speaks to me like that, I'm not used to it." Margaret didn't know how to have this kind of conversation, and she could only be honest. "Well, actually, one person did, but I thought she was just being kind."

"I assure you it's not kindness but the truth."

Just then a brilliant flash of lightning articulated the sky to the west. Margaret counted to eight before the thunder sounded. "My father says you count the seconds between the lightning and the thunder and then divide by five. That tells you in miles how close the lightning is. Less than two miles away, right over that hill," she said, pointing to a low rise on the other side of the road. "Exciting to have it so close, isn't it?"

"I'm not really thinking about the lightning." Nicholas looked at her blushing face, leaned over and kissed her mouth quickly. To his surprise, she returned the kiss with an ardour he hadn't expected. He put his arms around her and kissed her again under the dripping cottonwoods while the horses huddled nervously together nearby.

When the storm had passed and they rode their horses onto the Douglas Lake road, Margaret felt as though she carried it all inside her — the pungent smell of damp rocks and sage, the flowering buckwheat, the blackbird's shrill whistle, the warmth of the sun emerging from the back end of the thunderhead. Her mouth was remembering his mouth upon it, not like anything she'd ever known, yet she seemed to have waited her entire life to feel the texture of his lips, the pressure of his teeth. Nicholas was smiling at her, the blue of his eyes exactly like the bells of clematis that grew on the mountains.

She rode with him as far as the fork in the road where you could keep going to Douglas Lake or take a rougher trail up Hamilton Mountain. "You'll be fine now," she told him. "Just stay on the main road, and you'll be there before dark."

"Margaret!" He pulled his horse up beside hers and took one of her hands in his. "When will I see you next? Will you be able to ride with your father and me when he takes me to see the cattle?"

"I don't know. I'll see you when you come to meet with him, though." She was wondering how she could ride with them and not touch Nicholas, not hold his hand as she was now, their fingers laced together, unwilling to become two hands again, rest on the horns of their saddles as they moved away in separate directions, each hand at a loss unknown to it before.

The tea towels arrive, and with them a carefully written account of their making and a brief description of the manufacture of linen. I keep them wrapped in their tissue and enter their arrival in my ledger. I think of the woman's surprise at my welcoming such items for my exhibition and how little attention we pay to the archaeology of our own lives. Those reassembling our history will have such random scraps of our fabric. Photographs of isolated events, letters, a journal if we've been careful, a memory or two carried in the minds of our children.

When I travel to the Nicola Valley, it seems all of piece but protective of its stories. There are clues, of course — the community of graves in the Murray churchyard and the silent buildings in what's left of the townsite. The museum in Merritt has exhibits that offer a glimpse into the mining history, the ranching history, and enough objects to make me spend hours looking into glass cases where beaded gloves and newspapers repose alongside fossils and old harnesses. And there are buildings in Merritt that were there a hundred years ago, still bearing their dry siding and windows of wavy glass, one with a copper cupola. If I stand on the sidewalk and unfocus my eyes until I can just see their shapes, it's as if. As if.

Chapter Seven

A QUILT HAS COME, moving me to tears, an uncontained crazy quilt with a contained border. The pattern moves freely over the body of the quilt, the border follows a geometric pattern of control. A typewritten text accompanies the quilt, explaining that it had been pieced together with scraps of clothing from all the members of the maker's family who had died. Black velvet, faded brown corduroy, the heavy coarse worsted that fishermen's trousers are made of, tweed, gay flowered prints, the satin of fine gowns, tiny fragments of lace and the soft flannel of baby clothing, shards of fabric carefully fitted together, all framed with a three-inch-wide border composed of narrow strips of alternating colours of corduroy and worsted, looking for all the world like a stack of cordwood. The backing is pieced of sugar sacks, some of them plain and some faded prints. It is tied rather than quilted, tufts of grey wool threaded through at regular intervals. Staring at it, running my fingers over the lines of yellow feather-stitching outlining each scrap, feeling the soft nap of the velvet, the worn wales of the corduroy, I know that I am reading the map of a human heart. A cartography of grief and loss, a small remnant of pink flannel to indicate a baby daughter gone to an early grave, the constant black of the mourning clothes, the trousers of a husband lost at sea. The text is matter-of-fact but carefully records the date of each death and the provenance of each scrap: *Alice Jane Morris, died March 2, 1923, pieces of fabric from her summer dress; Rachel Mary Morris, died in childbirth,*

September 14, 1932, scrap of her wedding dress; Albert Thomas Morris, lost at sea and given up as drowned, herring, March 11, 1943, cloth taken from the cuff of his fishing pants. And then the text concludes with a fragment of hymn:

> *Riches I need not, nor man's empty praise,*
> *Thou mine inheritance, now and always,*
> *Thou and Thou only, first in my heart,*
> *High king of heaven, my treasure thou art.*

In Margaret's box, the postmarks on the letters form a map of another kind, cancellations of stamps in the tiny Spences Bridge post office, letters sent from the train station in Seattle, notes given to porters to mail as a train paused on a cold morning in Fargo, North Dakota, the early winter snow already falling. Letters from Astoria, telling of hair styles and books, new species of birds to be added to a life list kept in immaculate copperplate. In my mind, I flag each place in order to remember it as important when the map makes sense, is practical enough for my own journey.

And as for my own explorations of the valley, I have walked the road that she might have walked behind the Nicola River where the old grist mill would have been, I have driven to the Douglas Lake ranch, watched a golden eagle in contemplative flight over towards Hamilton Mountain. At a distance, someone on a horse, a dog at foot. In my pocket, a sprig of southernwood, its keen aroma keeping me alert to the country.

Everything at home had a dreamlike quality when Margaret returned. The grey pine fence-rails, the windows shining with late sun, the enamelled bucket by the barn pump, all of them luminous. She unsaddled Daisy and, before she turned her loose in the corral, kissed her neck again and again.

"He seems a nice fellow," her father commented as she entered the barn to put the saddle and bridle away. He'd seen her kissing her horse and hoped she hadn't noticed him smiling.

"Oh, yes," she replied.

William wondered what to say to her. She looked as though she was miles away, and he remembered the feeling well. The point about intense attraction was that it changed you forever, took you out of yourself to make possible all the years of work that made a marriage — building barns and raising children, living through difficulties, physical pain and occasional deep loneliness — that follow it logically as apples follow blossoms on a tree. The reasons that kept you connected to the object of that attraction remained true in their essence but altered, too, as bodies altered, as land changed over the years. But wasn't she too young for this? Jenny had been, what, eighteen when they'd met? He somehow imagined she'd been more ready for what happened than Margaret was, but he supposed that was what a father must think. And surely it was his responsibility to protect her from pain and grief as much as he could.

"Will you want to go up to the meadows with us when we go?"

"I'll have to talk to Mother first and make sure she won't be short-handed, but I'd love to go."

They fed the horses, and William handed Margaret the bucket of milk to take to the house. He remained in the barn, lighting a kerosene lantern when it got too dark to see what he was doing. Which was turning a broken rein over and over in his hands.

Those horses that came to our truck on the Pennask Lake road, heads low and eyes curious — it seemed they had something to say as they crowded around me while I stood in the autumn field with my paper bag full of apples. The one, the bay mare that I dream of, had eyes fringed with black lashes, eyes of deep beauty.

If there had been a way to speak to her, I wonder what I would have asked. Did a girl come this way, which tracks on this vast expanse of grass are hers?

They made a camp in a narrow cut between two ridges, some distance from the cow-camp. William wanted to use it as a base so that they could lighten the horses' loads and venture off to explore the higher country where the cattle spent their summers. There was a creek nearby for water and a pine that had been split open by lightning several years earlier; its fallen branches would make excellent firewood, dry and fragrant with pitch. Margaret had camped out with her father on many occasions and knew the way he liked to set up — big stones brought for a fire ring, tents in a sheltered area, horses tethered to sharp pegs but with plenty of room to graze. She shook out the saddle blankets and put hers in her tent to give her some protection against the hard ground. Jenny Stuart had packed stew in a sealer for their evening meal and some flour premixed with baking powder, to which they would add water and a lump of lard from their tin for bannocks. A half-dozen eggs, wrapped in pages of Eaton's catalogue, a slab of bacon, some cornmeal, two onions, dried beef, a bag of cut oats to make into porridge and to reward the horses. Most of the camping gear had been carried on the blue roan gelding, the best packhorse they owned.

The men were already fishing above the camp where the creek collected for a moment in a deep pool before tumbling off the edge of the hill in a sudden white fall. For some reason, the trout from these high creeks tasted better than those caught in lakes. The latter had softer flesh and something dank in their flavour, like waterweed. But these mountain trout, well, rainbows actually, had a flinty edge to their flesh, almost like granite. When

William came back to the camp with two of them carried by the gills on a stick, Margaret could already taste them, wrapped in thin slices of bacon to baste them and turned with an iron fork in the blue smoke of pine. She put a skillet underneath to catch their juices for flavouring the bannocks.

"Does this creek have a name?" asked Nicholas, watching the water race down the slope.

"Not really. There are a number of creeks this high, some of them only running when the snow melts. But this one is permanent, draining out of a lake without a name, farther up. Eventually it joins with another arm, and that creek runs into the Nicola River down towards our place. You know, I've fished all of the creeks, and there are some I'd swear have never seen a trout, but this one has always given me fish." As William spoke, he used his hatchet to slice a chunk of pine into pitchy sticks, wanting a quick hot flame to boil up a kettle of creek water for coffee.

When the fish were ready, Margaret divided them into equal portions on the tin plates and put a bannock on the plates, too. The fish was delicious, clean and sweet, and when they had finished every little morsel with their fingers, the stew was hot enough to ladle onto their plates. William made the coffee, adding the grounds to the kettle, letting it boil until it frothed over, removing the enamel pot briefly to a rock until the froth subsided, then repeating the procedure three more times. Margaret carefully placed the long backbone of each trout into the creek. Watching her, Nicholas imagined the pleasure of kissing her here on this golden hill, her mouth tasting of the trout and her hair smelling of the fire.

By now it was dusk. The fire settled into a comfortable burn, snapping now and again as hidden pitch ignited and flared. Margaret rinsed the plates and handed cups of coffee to the men. The stars were appearing in the clear sky, and William told Nicholas the names the Thompsons gave various constellations.

"Teit has material on this, I believe, so you'll come to it in your work. But it's useful to see the stars for yourself, in the country of the Thompsons, to get a sense of how they fit into the place. It might be easier to come up with French equivalents if you've seen what the Indians were referring to, physically if not spiritually."

The sky stretched out in every direction. "Follow that one bright star there directly in front of the big pine, yes, *there*. It's the Big Dipper, of course — my father called it the Plough — in Ursa Major. Well, here it's the Grizzly Bear. There's a story to go with it, you'll have to ask Margaret's grandmother for the details. And that one, just follow my hand exactly, yes, that's the one we call Cygnus, they call it the Swan, same thing, and they're very familiar with swans in this country. Colonies winter here on the plateau. The group right behind the Swan they think of as a canoe full of hunters pursuing the swan. It makes as much sense to me as anything else, maybe more than those old Greek stories. They trace their family trees back to the animals, you know. Some are descended from the coyote, some the antelope, others from badgers. And Coyote is the important animal here, really. He's a sort of an emblem, you could call him that, moving through this valley, changing people and other animals, birds, too, into bluffs and rock formations. He brought salmon to the Columbia River, brought them up the Fraser River into all the different feeder creeks and rivers."

They lay on their backs in dry grass by the fire. The stars were so many and so bright that Margaret covered her eyes with her right hand and peered up through the spaces between her three middle fingers. One constellation at a time, swans and hunters, tracks of the dead on the grey trail, a dog following the friends of the moon, one story that linked her to the vast sky which had been there when the earth was young and Coyote ranged across the valley in the company of grasses.

Later, in her tent, she listened for the breathing of the men in their own tent, their quiet voices murmuring in the darkness. Riding up here, she had felt that she might burst with joy,

Nicholas very close on one of August's horses, her father leading them up the rough cow trails through blossoming buckwheat and beargrass, their fragrant flowering tops swaying in the wind. She wondered if she'd be able to speak naturally or if her tongue would feel too thick for her mouth, the way it had in the kitchen on the day Nicholas had come for dinner. He, on the other hand, had been pleasant to her and her father, asking questions, doing his share of the work once they'd found the campsite, filling the kettle again and again so they always had water when they needed it. When they'd stopped for lunch, he'd caught her eye and smiled, saying quietly, "I'm glad you're here," and she felt that fire again, a charge of lightning running her spine, and in spite of the warmth of the day, she'd shivered.

They'd stopped for lunch by a slough, and on the reeds by the shore, a pair of red-winged blackbirds swayed on the tops of bulrushes. William tried to locate the nest but couldn't, the reeds grew too thickly and gave way to wild roses on the shore. Margaret leaned into the thicket of blossoming roses to inhale their sweet breath and saw the blackbirds' nest like a grassy cup on the stem of a bulrush, a single hatchling crouched baldly on the floor of the cup with three eggs still unhatched, like pale blue beans, mottled with green and darker blue. She backed away quietly and beckoned to the men, who came to peer in at them, the parents anxiously fluttering in the tangle of plants. Margaret pinched off a rosebud to tie into Daisy's forelock, and they resumed their meal of bread and cold beef.

"Everything is a little later up here," William commented. "The blackbirds around the ranch house have been feeding their young for a week or two now. And the roses down at Nicola Lake are nearly finished. Listen — a meadowlark! That'll be the male. Let's see if we can see him, the female will be on the nest, probably in those tussocks up on that ridge. Ah, yes, there he is!"

They looked to where William was pointing and saw the bright meadowlark, his yellow breast and throat bibbed in black.

"It's like flute music," said Nicholas in delight. "One of my sisters plays the flute, and she often practises a particular Bach sonata, I think it's in A minor, a beautiful clear piece. But no lovelier than that bird's song, I'd say."

And in her tent that night, Margaret remembered the thrill of hearing that visitor to Quilchena recite a Shakespeare sonnet. She had felt the same longing that day, the almost bitter joy the words left her with.

> *When proud-pied April, dressed in all his trim,*
> *Hath put a spirit of youth in everything,*
> *That heavy Saturn laughed and leaped with him,*
> *Yet nor the lays of birds, nor the sweet smell*
> *Of different flowers in odour and in hue . . .*

Now she had something, someone, to attach the longing to. She fell to sleep in its spell.

She had no idea at first why she woke but lay in her bedroll listening for clues. Random drops of rain fell on the canvas of her tent. Had they put the saddles under cover? She couldn't remember. She knew her father had rigged the food bags high in a tree; this was bear country, and they never forgot to remove food from temptation. Putting her jacket on over her under-clothes, she untied her tent opening and went out to check the site. Chances were this would only be a light rain as a cloud passed over the valley, high and transitory.

"Margaret?" Her father's voice came quietly from the other tent.

"I'm just checking to make sure the saddles are covered and there's nothing to be spoiled if the rain keeps up," she said softly. "There's no need for you to get up."

The horses were gathered under the biggest pine. By now it was raining harder, but it was fairly sheltered where the horses stood. Margaret could smell their bodies, warm and relaxed, and the odour of rain on pine needles, on pollen, on southern-wood and wormwood, on the smouldering logs in the fire, sizzling as each drop fell. She leaned against Daisy for a moment, her cheek on the horse's withers, her hair against the dark mane. That's what her father saw as he looked out of his tent opening to see why she was taking so long to return to her bed.

The next two days were fine and warm. William took Nicholas far and near, sometimes accompanied by Margaret (which tracks on the wide expanse might be hers?) and sometimes just the two men riding from the camp, each with a bannock wrapped in a clean handkerchief in his saddlebag. When they returned for supper the second evening, William had a pair of snared grouse hanging from his saddle by the feet. Margaret loved to eat grouse, willingly cooked them, but hated to clean them, so William took them aside and opened them up with a swift knife stroke down the centre of the abdomen. He quickly skinned them, removed all the entrails and buried them, after first carefully extracting the livers. He rinsed the body cavities in the creek, shaking out the excess water and blood. Taking his sharp knife, he split each bird down the backbone and flattened it so it would grill evenly over the fire.

"There you go, my dear. Mind you don't overcook the livers."

Margaret sharpened some cottonwood sticks and soaked them for a few minutes in water. Then she threaded them through the grouse, taking care to direct the sticks into meaty areas, four sticks per bird, reaching into the flesh to pull the sticks out the other end so that the bird was positioned in the middle. This made a kind of support rack so that Margaret could lay the ends of the sticks over one of the rocks ringing the fire and let the flattened grouse grill slowly over its heat. She turned them several times during the cooking, and when they were nearly done, she put sliced onions over the breast meat and covered them with the last few slices of bacon, once again catching the melting fat in the skillet to fry the bannocks. The livers were seared at the ends of two of the sticks, basted with a little bacon fat.

"I don't think I've ever tasted anything so delicious," Nicholas said, throwing the last clean bone into the fire. "You both are so accomplished! I *can* fish, my father took on the task of teaching me in his favourite river, the Ausable, near our summer place, so I don't suppose I'd go entirely hungry if I lived up here, but I can't say that I'd ever think of cooking the grouse the way you did. I'd probably end up with a charred lump that was still raw inside."

William laughed. "Well, I wasn't brought up to cook over fires like this, believe me, but I learned quickly enough the first summer I spent as a cowboy up on Roper's ranch on the Thompson. There were always camp cooks, but often we'd be out checking on cattle far from the camp, and we'd be given some beans to take along and maybe some flour. That was it, and you got pretty tired of beans and hard biscuits. There was one fellow I remember, he knew plants, and he'd cook grouse with wild onions and some peppery grass — I've never forgotten the taste of it, but I can't seem to find it here. Maybe it's the air that seasons the meat, too. I wonder how tasty this would be cooked in a skillet on a stove. Tough, maybe, and stringy."

"I'd say it would still taste wonderful," Nicholas replied. "But you say you weren't brought up to cook like this. Where do you come from?"

William told him about Astoria, his boyhood home on the shore of the Pacific. Margaret listened intently. When her father described that life, it was as though he was talking about someone else, a stranger, a boy from another world. Not the man she'd grown up with who knew horses, who loved the Nicola Valley with every fibre of his being. Yet she also remembered how tight and proper he'd become when his mother and sister had visited. Even his speech had changed, his vowels sounding more and more like theirs; his table manners, usually casual, had become, during that visit, an impossible model for his children. The way he held out the chair until his mother was seated, the way he held his fork, neatly wiped his mouth with his napkin — a stranger seemed to be eating at the ranch table. And there was a language between William and his mother, mostly unspoken, that Margaret had witnessed, as you might witness two people speaking Chinese; she had found it intriguing but impenetrable.

"It's ironic that I came up from Astoria to work on the Thompson Plateau because of all the stories I heard when I was young. The tales of David Thompson's explorations of the Columbia River were the ones that made me restless and eager to strike out on my own. The Indians called him the Star Man because of his interest in astronomy and mapping. I guess I thought that working my gillnetter would satisfy those feelings, but it wasn't what I needed."

Nicholas was engrossed. "Was the Thompson River named for him?"

"Yes, although he was never on it that I'm aware of. It was named by Simon Fraser, another explorer and a friend of David Thompson, and Thompson named the other great river after Fraser, who had made a journey down it, thinking it was the Columbia, until he reached the Pacific. I think I've got that right. A kind of exchange of honour, I suppose. My mother's father worked for John Jacob Astor's Pacific Fur Company at the original outpost back in the early part of the last century. I grew up hearing about these explorers, often from men who had known them or been on their expeditions. An old fellow who came to prune our trees each spring remembered seeing Thompson come into Astoria that day in 1811, he remembered the cedar canoe flying a British flag. He was only a boy, really, but it stayed with him, clear as anything."

"What did your own father do?" Nicholas asked, enjoying the conversation more than he could say. How right it seemed to be sitting by this fire with a girl he had kissed and her father, wanting to be nowhere else on earth.

"He had been a bar pilot on the Columbia River. There were two channels at the mouth, separated by a sand bar called Middle Sands, which kept changing as the sand shoaled in the storms and currents. He'd guide boats into the Columbia and out again, he knew the river like his own hands, knew about all the sandbars, which were navigable during particular tides, what conditions were likely to be through particular weathers. He never lost a boat and became something of a legend. Someone even composed a song in his honour, a sea-shanty that glorified one of his adventures in a Pacific squall."

Margaret exclaimed, "You've never told me that, Father! Can you remember the song?"

"Oh, not really. There was a refrain, let me see if I can get it right:

> *Captain Stuart brought her in, the limping broken beauty.*
> *No man died, though she'd a list to her side,*
> *And her sails hung all a-streaming.*

Perhaps not so much of a song after all."

"Could a man make a good living doing what your father did?"

"Well, he did very well financially, and my mother was left a considerable sum when her father died. My parents had a big house built on the slope overlooking the river, among the merchants and cannery owners. My sister and I were somewhat isolated in Astoria, though. She went to school in Portland after she turned twelve, and I had a tutor because I made such a fuss about going away to school. There wasn't much society in Astoria, and our parents had made our lives conspicuously different from those around us. I could escape occasionally, going up the river by canoe, alone or with another boy, as far as I could reach by water, then walking the riverbanks to see the fishing platforms at Celilo and to look at the Indian villages where the Klickitat River flowed into the Columbia, and the Wind, farther west. I guess I wanted to see where the fish I'd missed catching ended up, some of them hanging on grey latticed racks to dry in the sun, some being roasted on fires as I passed the camps. Some people said that runs of them travelled as far

as the Snake River and even farther, into the Salmon River.
Fishing gave me people to work with, the men who helped me
figure out settings and how to care for my boat gave me
companionship, but I think my sister was disadvantaged by too
much of one thing and not enough of others."

"Did she stay in Astoria, or did she do something as interesting
as you?"

William laughed. "Interesting is not the half of it, Nicholas.
She was sent to Boston for finishing but never married. She lives
with my mother, still in the big house, still with servants and
proper standards, as they would have it. They came here for two
months a couple of years ago, their first and only trip to Canada,
although they go to Europe regularly and to the east coast fairly
often. Father left them very well off and left me a substantial
amount of money, too, although he wouldn't write to me once
I'd settled here, wouldn't acknowledge me."

Then William was quiet, remembering the loneliness of that
break with his family. It was a wonder to him that he'd come so
far from his original home and found such happiness, undreamed
of in the earliest years. He had loved the vast country he'd
travelled through to get to the Thompson Plateau, the openness
of the sky, even the cryptic messages rattlesnakes left in the sand.
He felt he could breathe deeply after years in the fog, his lungs
filling with dry air and the pollen of the grey herbs settling on
his body as he rode the benchlands and side valleys. In his socks,
the hooked seeds of barley and wild grass.

At Margaret's bidding, Nicholas told them something of his
life in New York City, where his father practised law and his
mother tried to grow apples and roses in their garden.

"When my mother was a child, she was taken to Versailles,
and she was captivated by the Orangerie and then, at Malmaison,
by the roses of the Empress Josephine. I think she missed her
calling, she should have been one of those grand ladies of
horticulture. Instead she fell in love with my father when he came
to France on a holiday and married him. Father was ready to

leave Dublin at that time anyway because there were so few opportunities for Catholics, the country was run by Anglo-Irish, although Father said many of them hadn't seen England in generations. So they came to New York, and Mother resigned herself to raising what she could, children and flowers, in the sooty air of our back garden.

"Why did he choose New York? I thought Boston was the main destination for Irish immigrants."

"Well, New York had a large Irish population, his cousins had come earlier to study medicine, so it was a natural choice for him, I suppose. My sisters and I were born there, of course, but both sets of grandparents are still alive, my mother's parents in Chantilly and my father's in Dublin, and we've made two trips to Europe to visit them. I loved Ireland and hope to spend more time there when I've finished my university work."

Margaret, who had never been farther than Spences Bridge and Kamloops, had a sudden yearning for Versailles and even Astoria, where her aunt Elizabeth was that very moment working on a sampler with a verse from Psalms. *As for man, his days are as grass: as a flower of the field, so he flourisheth, For the wind passeth over it, and it is gone; and the place thereof shall know it no more.* Around the edges, she was stitching clumps of bunchgrass in soft gold and green.

When the trio rode down off the mountain the next afternoon, in their saddlebags a blackened skillet and bedrolls that needed an afternoon in a good wind to freshen them of woodsmoke and dust, August was waiting to tell William that the new mare was in heat.

"Are you certain, August? Have you teased her?"

Nicholas looked shocked that William would ask his brother-in-law such a thing, so William quickly explained the strategy to find if a mare was really fertile. A stallion would be led near her but on the other side of a partition, and her response and the stallion's would be assessed: did her tail rise, did her opening twitch and contract, did she repeatedly urinate, did she squat, was she uncharacteristically aggressive? Was the stallion interested? The stallion used for this was not the Bonny Prince but a lesser stud, one that was generally turned loose with the range mares during the breeding season, and August reported that Thistle had squealed and showed all the positive signs of estrus, almost sitting in front of the stallion with her hindquarters toward him. August offered to stay with William rather than going home immediately as he'd planned if William wanted to go ahead with the breeding.

While the men discussed the agenda for the meeting of Thistle and the Bonny Prince, Margaret went to the barn to visit the mare. She was in one of the roomy box stalls, at the opposite end of the barn from the stallion. She was damp with sweat and kept moving from one side of her stall to the other, breathing heavily and showing the whites of her eyes as Margaret approached her. She let her neck be stroked and listened nervously as Margaret spoke gentle words in her ear, telling her how she'd love the trip up Hamilton Mountain, maybe next year when her foal was weaned. If there was a foal. Occasionally a mare would miscarry or give birth to a stillborn foal or else have such difficulty with the delivery that the foal would be sacrificed to save her. Or the other way around, depending on the amount of damage.

As Margaret started for the house with her bag of camping gear to sort and clean, her father called to her. They would introduce the two horses in the next hour, since there were enough strong men around to assist, and he'd need her help, too. Could she make sure her mother could spare her?

I have driven to Astoria with my family in the wet spring weather, looking to find something that I had no name for — a glimpse, a flicker in the trees. On the road from Longview to the bridge at the mouth of the Columbia, I knew I was approaching the answer to the riddle of a life abandoned suddenly, on a morning in autumn, a note left at dawn, the girl who would come, in time. Through Grays Harbour and Skamokawa, detouring to look at a covered bridge in farmland where a three-legged dog raced our truck to the narrow entrance, where cattle stood up to their slim ankles in mud. A boy drifted in a red canoe on Grays River towards the dark Willapa hills, not noticing us as we paused to take our bearings.

I remember stately houses in Astoria, turreted, pilastered, standing serene in the rain on the slope of land overlooking the river. A boy walking up from the river, the memory of high waves and calmer swells in his gait, fish scales drying on his hands. We followed directions to the Astoria Column, modelled after Trajan's Column in Rome and decorated with events celebrating the winning of the West, "commemorating the westward sweep of discovery and migration which brought settlement and civilization to the Sunset empire." It looked like an enormous penis atop the aptly named Coxcomb Hill, and that in itself was symbolic of the westward sweep of migration — though hardly discovery — which brought smallpox, venereal disease, fishing restrictions, loss of land, and ultimately a kind of extinction to the original inhabitants of that Sunset empire.

The next morning, still hoping for a glimpse of a life, a notion, we went to the Columbia River Maritime Museum, chronicling two hundred years of ships and history. I found the boats haunting, the gillnetters rigged and positioned in the great hall, their planks dry and gaping after too many years of indolence, the pieces of shipwreck, harpoons from the whaling boats poised in their cases. Who would have given up a boat to stand uselessly in a hall, its very ribs longing to feel the breaking of a wave, its planks dried forever of blood and scales, the solace of kelp. You could almost smell the salmon, but the woman in the shop told me there was no longer a fishery, and little wonder when I remembered the dams upriver, the early ones lacking even fish ladders, the fish throwing themselves against the enormous concrete faces and dying with their bodies full of eggs, the fish-wheels at The Dalles that "scooped salmon from the river by the ton."

At the small museum of quilts and textiles, I talk to the curator about climate control and insect damage and examine the collection. Wonderful quilts from the women who came west over the Oregon Trail, the pattern names singing a ballad of migration — Wandering Foot, Flying Geese, a variant of Drunkard's Path called Oregon Trail, Birds in Flight, Star and Compass — and echoes of hardship in the fabrics themselves: mourning prints and the tiny scraps of dresses worked into crazy quilts.

We didn't go on the walking tour of heritage houses (and anyway, would he have been there in a window, a boy behind a hedge, a shadow turning in a swing?) because it wouldn't stop raining. Only for a few minutes, while we were looking out from the top of the Astoria Column, did the rain let up enough for us to see how the town stood in relation to the Pacific and the rivers feeding into the Columbia. It was as though the town ended suddenly and completely just southwest of where we leaned over the railings, the forests taking over and the rivers winding their way back like grey silk to the skein of their watersheds. No roads or settlements that I could see to punctuate the green expanse, no organized farmland. I'd read David Thompson's journals of his trip down the Columbia and knew that his Astoria entries were mild observations of weather and the manners of Mr. Astor's company. I wonder if he came to Coxcomb Hill, on a day such as "July 17 Tuesday A very fine day" or "July 19 Thursday A fine hot day" and looked at this same view. He'd have noted co-ordinates and wind direction, but I wonder if he looked at the quattrocento gathering of rivers and felt where he was, not in terms of longitude and latitude, but in eternity, and if he felt as though he'd arrived, finally, after years in canoes and winter camps. Or whether he thought only of the next turn in undiscovered rivers, waiting to be drawn in and correlated, the sound of them gathered in quiet pools near where a man might sleep in the open, dreaming of another life.

Chapter Eight

ITEMS CONTINUE TO COME IN, and I enter each in my book and make a plan for its display, taking into consideration the condition of the piece and what it has to say about its maker and use. To my delight, an elderly Native woman brought in several baskets and spent a few hours telling me about their making. Two were her own work and a third had been made by her mother. One was made of slough sedge and imbricated with a design of cherry bark and maidenhair fern stems, representing the long canoes of the area. Another was an open-work basket of cedar withes, used for clams and other things that might drain as you carried them. The one I liked best was a beautiful basket of coiled spruce root, generous and wide and so tightly woven it could be used to carry water. And in speaking of the baskets, the woman shared with me the narrative of women's work, which had more than a little to do with the marriage of beauty and utility. I thought of how her hands had been shaped by her mother's hands to harvest and prepare the materials for baskets, to shape them and decorate them and preserve them. And how the hands of the women who'd embroidered the tea towels, pieced together fabric for quilts, dyed and printed plain cottons for clothing, had in turn been shaped by their mother's hands. The shadows of our mothers and grandmothers are forever over our shoulders, their arms over ours, their hands ready to help us find our way in the materials.

"Father wants me to help with the mare, Mother. I know I've just come in, but can you spare me? I'll clean up the camping gear when we're finished outside."

Jenny was agreeable, wanting only to know how the camping had gone. She told Margaret to let the others know there would be food when they were finished.

At the barn, William and August were getting the equipment for the covering together. Because they were uncertain how Thistle would behave during the mating, they were going to use a twitch and hobbles, and these were brought out to the breeding chute. William asked Margaret to prepare Thistle, since the mare was accustomed to the girl saddling her. He had a bucket of warm water ready and a length of clean cotton for wrapping her tail. Margaret carefully bound the upper portion of the black tail, talking and stroking the tense muscles of Thistle's rump and back while she did so. Then, once the tail was bound, she carefully washed the mare's haunch and vulva. She would be holding Thistle during the mating, trying to keep her calm and cooperative.

Outside, William had the stallion haltered with the breeding halter, which had a special band that could drop to put pressure on the Prince's sensitive nose if he needed to be restrained. He had been washed with warm water and was clearly excited as he waited near the chute, dancing around, his upper lip lifting and twitching as he smelled Thistle in the air. Twice he gave a high-pitched scream that had the range stallion screaming back from a corral on the other side of Culloden.

William led the stallion away while Margaret walked Thistle into the breeding chute, August waiting to help her with the hobble and twitch. A flock of magpies had gathered on the big cottonwood near the barn, muttering and eager not to miss a thing. Later Margaret would remember the way everything was washed with golden light, as thick and limpid as honey. Each sound was articulated clearly — the chickens clucking as they made their way into the shed, one of the dogs groaning as he scratched an ear with his hind paw, the crows calling as they flew above Culloden on their way to some new carrion.

Margaret brought Thistle right up to the bar. The horse was nervous, but still she let August fasten the hobble from her near front foot to her off hind foot. Then he gently applied the twitch to her upper lip while she tossed her head until Margaret brought it down and held it steady. August put the neck guard over her shoulders, adjusting it so that her withers were covered, buckling it under her neck.

"What's that pad for?" asked Nicholas, who had come to the front of the chute in case Margaret needed help to hold Thistle.

"Stallions usually keep their balance with their teeth while mating. This way, he can grab the guard and not poor Thistle. We know what he'll be like for this, but not her. I feel bad about putting all these restraints on her when I think she'll be fine, but it would terrible if she kicked the Prince or one of us. She seems so anxious."

"She's had foals," commented August, "so she's not maiden. This won't be new to her."

William was bringing the stallion to the chute now, the horse prancing and snorting eagerly on the lead. He was well-trained and didn't ignore his handler, but he was fully drawn and eager to mount Thistle. William brought him to the near side of the breeding chute to tease the mare and prepare her. She urinated and then lifted her tail, almost sitting down as she moved her rump back and forth. The stallion's neck steamed with sweat, and he was blowing hard as he entered the chute, William helping him to mount the waiting mare and to position his penis at her opening by lifting her bound tail right back. August released Thistle's hobble so that she could brace herself under the stallion's great weight.

"Could you hold her head a little higher?" William asked, and Margaret lifted the mare's head, speaking calmly to her as she did so. Thistle's chest pushed hard against the bar and the stallion repeatedly thrust into her, August and Nicholas helping to steady her and keep her as still as they could. The Bonny Prince snorted and grunted, rolling his eyes, as he thrust violently against Thistle's damp rump. Margaret held her breath as she felt the weight of the two bodies driving against the breeding chute. The stallion was gripping the neck cover with his teeth, his mouth was so close that Margaret could see where the long teeth left his gums, the fierce strength with which they clenched the leather. Yet there was beauty in his great shape covering the sweating mare, his shoulder muscles rippling with the exertion of his movements and his jugular groove contracting. And then it was over, William was backing him off to the mare's near side and swinging him away from her hindquarters, then leading him away to cool down before taking him back to the barn.

August quietly removed Thistle's twitch and neck-cover and took the loosened hobble from her foot. She was trembling, and Margaret backed her out of the chute, leading her down to walk along the creek. Nicholas walked beside them, quiet after the drama of what had taken place, wondering at the shock and radiance of the huge bodies moving together in that narrow space between weathered boards. He brushed a fly off Margaret's arm and felt her flinch.

"I'm sorry, I didn't mean to startle you."

"It's fine, you surprised me, that's all. I wonder if Thistle is cool enough to put away now. My mother wanted you to come in for something to eat before you left."

"I've never seen anything like that before," said Nicholas, still thinking of the horses. "I had no idea how involved a process horse-breeding is. I suppose I just thought horses would be turned out in privacy, not brought together like that. Do you always help?"

Margaret looked at him steadily and replied, "Well, Nicholas, as you saw, several people are needed, and I'm the likely one, aren't I? Our range horses are allowed to mate in privacy, as you put it, but with the Bonny Prince and Thistle, we have a big investment, and we can't take the chance of one of them getting injured."

He realized that she'd taken his comment as criticism of her complicity in the procedure, and that was not what he had intended. She was murmuring to the horse now, telling her they'd go to the barn and get her some oats and a bucket of water. She didn't look at him.

"Margaret, I only meant that I keep finding out how little I know about anything, even relations among horses. Please don't think I was questioning how your father manages his ranch. I thought you were both marvellous, the way you knew exactly what to do, and how you were so matter-of-fact about everything. I'm twenty-two years old, the product, you might say, of a fine university, and I must confess I was somewhat embarrassed when that stallion approached your mare. The universities don't even pretend to touch on life, it seems."

She smiled at his admission. "On a ranch we see more than most people, I suppose. I think my father might be unusual, too, because he's always assumed I would help with these things, and he hasn't felt it would hurt my character to see animals doing what it is in their nature for them to do. But I was embarrassed, too, today. I thought I was going to cry at one point, I can't really say why."

She was looking at him over the halter rope, shy again as she had been in the kitchen, at the marsh, on the road to Spahomin with the blooming bitterroot between them. He leaned forward to kiss her mouth, his hand on Thistle's neck for balance. They returned the horse to the barn, Nicholas going to the pump to fill a bucket with water while Margaret scooped oats out of the feed room and rubbed the horse down with a soft cloth to soothe her. Unwrapping the mare's tail, Margaret used an end of the cotton to wipe a stream of mucous from her inner flank. Closing the stall door, Margaret led Nicholas to the warm kitchen, where William and August were sitting at the table, eating hot biscuits and fried chicken. After their meal, the men sat on the porch in the dusk, drinking a dram of whiskey while Margaret helped her mother to put away food and wash dishes. The bats were coming out, darting between barn and cotton-woods, where a new hatch of mayflies hovered in the gilded air. Two nighthawks hunted over Culloden, their shrill cry and buzz, cry and buzz sounding over the ranch yard. And in a small corral, the stallion that had not been given the opportunity to mate with Thistle voiced his frustration to the first stars.

After August and Nicholas had left to ride back to Spahomin, Margaret scoured the skillet and plates from the camping trip. She took kitchen leavings out to the chickens and listened for coyotes. She could hear horses stirring in their stalls; the roan gelding in the yard neighed once for reasons known only to him, and the Bonny Prince answered. It was lonely to be the only one standing in the yard, listening to the world going on in its intimacy. Margaret returned to the house and said her goodnights to her parents. Then she took a jug of warm water to her room. Tipping the water into her wash-bowl, she took off her shirt and chemise and washed her arms and breasts, using a bar of scented soap she'd been given by her Astoria grandmother ("Hard milled with the flowers of Provence"), drying herself with a rough towel that smelled of spring air. She washed her ankles, her feet and her knees. Taking off her underpants, she crouched over the bowl to wash between her legs. The warm water felt welcome. Margaret also felt something else, a feeling she didn't have a word for, but suddenly she knew how Thistle had felt in the hours before the stallion mounted her. She must have yearned for him, the consolation of his body in the golden air, waited for him, restless in her solitude. Was this what the poets meant when they spoke of longing, this physical ache which felt like hunger and pain, like the beautiful complicity of fire?

Nicholas was glad that August was a man of few words as they rode home in the darkness, the horses jogging surely on the dusty road. He was full of astonishment at the way this sojourn was unfolding beyond any expectation he could have had. He was beginning to think he had fallen in love, not just with the girl he had left behind in her mother's kitchen, but with the entire valley. After they'd unsaddled the horses and made conversation with Alice, August's wife, Nicholas read a little by the light of his kerosene lamp and worked on his notes. Moths fluttered around in the weak light, and one or two entered the transparent chimney, briefly flaring, then turning to soot against the glass. Lying on his back, he thought of Margaret riding down from the hill in starlight that first night; he remembered kissing her while summer lightning crackled in the sky. He had known girls before, the daughters of his father's associates or the sisters of classmates at Groton, then Columbia. He'd escorted them to parties, the opera, for Sunday outings to the Brooklyn Botanical Gardens, making witty conversation by the roses. Yet none had made as singular an impression as the sight of Margaret Stuart, her hair dishevelled and her clothing dusty, cooking grouse over a fire of sweet pine. Or holding Thistle steady while the stallion copulated with her, bracing himself with his teeth. Nicholas turned his face into the pillow and said her name to the darkness, quietly.

Nicholas received permission from William to take Margaret to a dance in the Nicola hall the next weekend; they would go with August and Alice and their oldest daughter, Eliza. William provided the buggy, August driving it to Spahomin the day before the dance, and it had been arranged that Margaret would be collected late in the afternoon. She had hung her rose-coloured dress in her window that morning so that the creases could ease out during the day. Her mother heated the sad-irons on the stove and helped her to press it, the kitchen redolent of damp muslin and steam. Margaret washed herself and brushed out her hair, dabbing a little of Aunt Elizabeth's perfume from Grasse on her wrists and the hollow of her neck. She was very excited and nervous, never having attended a dance without her family and certainly not on the arm of a young man.

When the buggy came up the dusty lane, Margaret was

waiting on the porch. Nicholas jumped from his seat and ran up the steps.

"You look beautiful! What a lovely dress! And what have you done to your hair?"

Margaret smiled. She had brushed it, that's all, and run a piece of silk over it to settle it. Had he thought she would be waiting in her riding clothes to be taken to the dance? She let him help her up into the buggy, where her relations were dressed in their finest, too, and waving goodbye to the children watching their sister in awed silence from the rope swing under the cottonwoods, she said a little prayer to herself that the evening would be perfect.

And it was. Jack Thynne was there with his banjo, two men had fiddles, and the music was wonderful. Margaret had been to these fetes all her life and knew the various dances that the musicians would play, the Virginia reel, a Spanish waltz, a polka, one man calling the dances so everyone would know what to do next. Nicholas had never been to this kind of dance and was amazed at the skill expected of all the dancers, the way groups dancing the quadrille would move from one partner to the next in perfect rhythm. During one of the breaks, he and Margaret went outside to get a breath of air. Standing a little way from the hall, he could hear loons on Nicola Lake and coyotes yipping very near. He imagined writing a letter home to describe how one moment he was dancing and the next listening to coyotes outside the hall, the stars so many and so close that they dusted the cheeks and shoulders of the girl he was with, and he wondered what his family would make of it.

"Margaret, may I ask you a question?"

"Of course."

"That first afternoon I met you, I said something about the train robbers, and you got angry and said I didn't understand. I got the impression you knew something about the capture that you didn't want anyone else to know. Was I right?"

They had walked away from the hall by then, along the main

road towards the Driard Hotel. Every window was lit, and from the road Nicholas and Margaret could hear two men talking quietly on the upper balcony, saw the glow of their cigarettes and heard the clink of glass as something was poured from a bottle. Margaret told him the story then, in a rush, of riding to Chapperon Lake that morning, quietly moving to the edge of the camp and seeing the three men with their simple meal by the campfire, the others confronting them with accusations, the gunfire, the scream of the man who was shot in the leg.

"You must have been terrified!" Nicholas could scarcely imagine what it must have been like for her to come upon the drama as she had, unknowing, a girl on a horse in a remote place.

"I rode away as fast as I could, I didn't really know what it had all been about until later, when the story of the capture began to be told by everyone, but I really thought that George Edwards was innocent. Now it seems he actually did rob trains. I read the newspapers in Kamloops and listened to the accounts of the trial, the first trial and then the retrial just last week, but I still find it hard to think of him as dangerous. He isn't, wasn't, a bad man, not really. How could he be, when everyone, including my father, liked him and trusted him? When he was on his way by train to prison in New Westminster, a woman saw him who said he'd spent a night in her home. This was in the newspaper only yesterday. Lots of us have something like that to say about him — we knew him, liked him, thought of him as just like any other man. And the story of the capture makes the scouting team sound brave beyond belief. But they were the ones who ambushed three men while they were eating and then shot wildly everywhere, not Edwards and the other two. Anyway, I just couldn't talk about it to anyone because I knew how worried my parents would be if they knew I'd been there. It was like a bad dream, Nicholas, and I have even dreamed of it since, often. I wake up with the awful feeling that there's no one to tell. It's such a relief to tell you, but you must promise you won't say anything to my father."

"But were you frightened when you realized what was happening?"

"Oh, yes, I was. I remember getting off my horse and trying to calm myself by lying down in the grass. I could hear my heart beating, it sounded like a drum. I couldn't believe at first that no one had seen me, I kept expecting the police, although I didn't know then that's who they were, to come after me at a gallop, but I guess there was such confusion at the campfire that no one noticed me or heard my horse's hooves as we left."

Nicholas put his arm around her shoulder and drew her to his side. His own heart was racing as she told the story, and he was surprised at her courage. "Did you follow the trial closely?"

"I think everyone did. We went to Kamloops just a day after the preliminary hearing to attend a concert — my father had arranged the trip long before. The newspapers were full of it, and my father asked his friend the stage driver to leave newspapers for him twice a week at the crossroads so he could read all about the trial without having to go all the way to Nicola. There was a joke, 'Bill Miner is not so bad, he only robs Canadian Pacific Railway every two years, but the CPR robs us every day.' I thought of him being taken into Kamloops in the rain, I could see it in my mind so clearly, the wagon bringing the men to the jail on Seymour Street in the streaming rain, the street muddy, bells ringing them in, the light grey and electric at the same time. They were soaking wet and wrapped in blankets, wearing handcuffs, Mr. Edwards in the front with the second man and the one who was shot lying in the back. I could even smell the mud and the wet horses. I heard some of this in Kamloops and read some of it — I feel as if I was there, but I wasn't, really."

Thinking of her walking in the darkness alongside a hotel that no longer exists apart from its image on sepia cards which

I pin to my wall, hoping for a trick of the light to show me her shadow among those cast by slender pines, I want so much to hear her telling her story to the young man at her side. What will come to them, in the fullness of years, is sorrow, and I would take it upon myself if I could. *Give unto them beauty for ashes, the oil of joy for mourning, the garment of praise for the spirit of heaviness.* No one who has walked in darkness in the ardour of youth knows that the garment of praise is so easily put aside. Or that the spirit of heaviness, once taken on, is a weight on the shoulders forever after, a burden to be borne even during times of great joy. Or that what is remembered of a life fades to a few photographs, a receipt for train travel, some dates carved in stone propped up in a graveyard among cactus and stunted iris. In dry air, magpies remember the dead; wind carries seed from one field to another.

They returned to the dance to the opening strains of a waltz. Holding her, Nicholas reflected on how uneventful his own life had been compared to Margaret's thus far, and yet he had sailed to Europe, attended lectures by world-renowned scholars and philosophers, travelled by train across the breadth of America. After the waltz, Archie Kelly, one of the fiddlers, announced that he would play a suite of reels from his native Ireland. The other musicians sat back and listened as he lifted his fiddle and played so swiftly, so uncannily sweetly, that no one danced, no one clapped, but stood in the spell of "Scotch Mary," "The Dunmore Lassies" and "Robbers Glen." How ironic, thought Margaret, that there would be a piece of music about the moment at Chapperon Lake before the lawmen arrived on the scene. At midnight, the ladies brought out the supper: platters of cold beef and thin slices of cured ham; baskets of high biscuits, split and filled with sweet butter; slices of pound cake and apple pie and heaps of airy meringues dusted with sugar; urns of tea and coffee, pitchers of lemonade with slivers of ice, and ginger beer. Some of the men went outside to share swallows of rum from flasks they concealed in the buggies, in the wood pile, in the bushes. More dancing followed the supper, and at dawn the Stuart-Jackson buggy headed home along the road that clung to the hillside above the lake, Alice and Eliza asleep on the seat beside August, Margaret and Nicholas holding hands under the blanket that was hardly needed, the air still warm and dry, Venus hanging on the horizon like a tiny brilliant lamp.

The stallions of the valley run through memory, The Boss, The King of Nicola, Rothesay Castle, Bonaparte Denmark, Galloway Prince, Diamond Fire, the generations raised by John Chilihilsa and sent to the Front in France, Woodward's Peppy San, some branded with the three bars of Douglas Lake, some with the curved line over a straight from Guichons, the JL of the Lauder Ranch, the inverted V followed by an X from the Jackson Ranch, T of the Willow, and the Cottonwood's half-circle with a trailing line to represent William's lost gillnetter, its net out for salmon in a glittering sea.

And I have been examining the buckskin jacket, unwrapping it carefully from its tissue. It is so soft to the touch that I want to rub my cheeks against the sleeves. It smells warmly of skin with a recollection of sage, either from the bark woven into the fringe or the smoke used for its curing, smudges that might be ash or fine dust. And it smells of lavender, too, from the little sachet tucked into its tissue. I spend a long time just looking at it, meditating on its empty sleeves, its toggles of horn. What do textiles remember of their makers, the deft touch of their fingers, and do they carry the shape of the bodies who have worn them, the heavy absence of shoulders or the pressure of a spine? In one of the photographs there is a child dressed in buckskin leggings and an overshirt, not one of the fair children in their Sunday best, but a small girl, her black hair braided, serious eyes, and the tiniest of smiles on her lips. Beauty for ashes and a garment of praise.

Chapter Nine

SORTING AND ARRANGING, preparing and restoring; the artifacts begin to fill the small room I've set aside for preparing them. More tea towels arrive, immaculately laundered, their embroidered proverbs faded but perfectly stitched. And more quilts, a cedar cape from an elderly storekeeper who once took it in trade for tinned milk, a wedding dress made in a remote logging camp for a cook who was marrying a faller and sent up by steamship, a beaded purse, beautiful cotton sheets with fields of wildflowers delicately knotted and feather-stitched along an eyelet border, needlepoint pillow covers, sweaters knitted out of the rough, unwashed wool so beloved of those working in the weather because of its ability to hold in warmth and shed water, baby dresses smocked and pleated, more samplers, including one stitched by a child, with a log cabin overlooked by a sombre moon and a whimsical alphabet. I think of the hands, all the hands, stitching and knitting and folding and smoothing, hands shaping as they cut and turned the fabrics, fitting to bodies, adjusting, by daylight and lamplight. In this room, I seem to be assisted by ghosts as I make my entries, plan and arrange, their hands palpable but unseen, a weight on my own as I fold and smooth.

July passed in the usual way, William attending to the cattle, Jenny to the children and garden, Margaret between them and useful to both. Nicholas Byrne returned to Spences Bridge to work with Mr. Teit and sent a letter:

It is hot here, the sides of the canyon are like oven walls, but the orchards are lovely and green. I like to walk among the trees at dawn while the sprinklers are going. Everything feels cool and alive. I've seen my first rattlesnake. It was reclining in a box of Mrs. Smith's peaches, easily four feet long and with an extraordinary rattle. It looked as though it was sleeping, but then it flicked its tongue in our direction. I'll never forget the odour of it mixed with the perfume of ripe peaches. The man who helps with the irrigation removed it from the crate with a stick and cut off its head. It was fascinating to touch the snake, minus its head, of course, and to discover how dry the skin was. I expected it to be slimy, or damp, at least. I could smell it on my hands for some time after. There has been so much to do, both with Mr. Teit and in getting my bearings in this area.

A fellow took me to see the devastation left behind after a mountain slide last year. Apparently the river was completely dammed after a side of the mountain came down and landed on the Indian village across the river. A train was about to pass through but luckily stopped in time. Passengers on the train saw people and animals being swept along in the torrent of water and mud but couldn't do anything to help. I think that would be terrible beyond imagining. But you must know of this landslide, I'm sure. I've met the new chief, Charles Walkem, and have found him to be a very genial fellow, very keen to rebuild and prosper. He introduced me to the woman who makes baskets, and she is a lot like your grandmother, although I don't think her baskets are quite so fine. She has told me lots of stories, one about a sort of war between fishes and another about Grizzly Bear's grandchild. Each evening I scramble up the mountain above the Murray Creek and look down at the town, with its rivers meeting and rushing down to the Canyon. Once I came back down with a herd of bighorn sheep, and I was amazed at their agility, running down the gravelly slope while I was trying to find a toehold that wouldn't slide away under me.

How are you? I think of you always, imagining you riding your horse along that lovely river. I will come back as soon as I'm able to.

Reading the letter, Margaret remembered the news of the landslide coming to them last year from Spences Bridge. One of her grandmother's cousins had married into the Cook's Ferry band and had attended service in the new Anglican church. Walking home after the service, the group she was with saw the water rushing their way, and they scrambled to higher ground. Those who had lingered at the church, those who had remained in their houses, and children who were playing by the river were washed away. Margaret's grandmother had been very sad at the news and told her that some believed the tribe was doomed to extinction and might see this as part of the end. An entire group of wintering Thompsons had been killed by smallpox years earlier, very near to where the Cook's Ferry slide occurred. Grandmother Jackson felt it must have been an unlucky place to build a village. Yet Margaret had been to Spences Bridge with her father and had stood on the banks of the Thompson River where the Nicola swirled into it, seen the remnants of fish camps all along the shore, even a few kikulis on higher ground. She thought the location was beautiful. Mountains rising from either side of the canyon, threaded with creeks and waterfalls coming down off the cliffs like liquid silver. The air was intense and dry, pungent with sage. She could actually smell the rivers, too — the familiar Nicola with its edge of snow from its high watershed past Barton Lake, the Thompson with its flinty nose of benchlands and rattlesnakes. Margaret had been hoping to see a rattlesnake, but it was still too early for them to come out of their dens on the talus slope, though she found the sun very warm — it was early March — and watched the grass expectantly anyway.

Once Nicholas did come, but Margaret had gone with one of the Nicola ladies to Kamloops by stage for a few days. When she returned home, she was bitterly disappointed to find out she had missed his visit. It had been brief, and he'd had to return to Spences Bridge to meet with Dr. Charles Newcombe, who was travelling up from Victoria to purchase some baskets and clothing that Mr. Teit had accumulated. He left a letter for her with Jenny and promised to come again soon. Margaret went for a ride that evening, letting Daisy gallop until she was quite damp with sweat and then cooling her down by a creek that made its way down the hill to meet with the Nicola River. Margaret sat in the dry grass and let Daisy graze, holding the reins in her right hand while she wiped at tears with her left. She had never felt so lonely in her life, although the only thing that had changed was her meeting with Nicholas, and he was gone, so oughtn't she to feel as she had before he came? It was hard to fathom how a person could feel so bereft and lonesome, just because another was absent. It was not only that he was far away but that there was no possibility of an evening visit, even though there hadn't been many: the sight of dust rising on the Douglas Lake road and then the sound of his horse on the lane. Or the knowledge that he was sleeping just a few miles away, under the same sky, the same moon in its house over him. She wondered if her mother and father felt this way when her father was away in the cowcamps or the branding camps for weeks at a time. Her mother always seemed busy and never cried. Yet she was quiet in the evenings and given to looking out windows at the black night. She often prepared his favourite foods and told the children as they were eating, "Your father loves these biscuits, I hope he's eating well."

While Margaret sat in the grass, she remembered how she had once felt the presence of the young girl here among the rocks and dry earth, and she wondered if the girl had longed for a particular young man, made excuses to be around him, watched him under shy lashes at communal events. Margaret hoped she hadn't died without feeling the sharp catch of her breath in her throat when the boy caught her eye or brushed against her. She took solace in the fact that she was alive to feel these things, not buried with a necklace of elk teeth and a drinking tube she would never use. She'd kept the drinking tube after cleaning it carefully, she'd even used it to drink from the Nicola River; how odd it had felt to taste the living water coming up through the ancient length of bone, flakes of calcium coming away against her palate. She kept it on the windowsill in her bedroom, a charm to be held and wondered at on nights when, sleepless, she stood looking at the stars. Had the girl's mouth ever touched the surface, had her tongue probed the opening, wearing the rough edges smooth over time?

The whole family helped with haying, moving up to the hay camp for its duration, while Jenny's sister Josie stayed at the ranch house to feed the chickens and pigs, milk the cow, and keep an eye on Thistle and the Bonny Prince. The hay camp was fun for the younger children, they were allowed to sleep in tents and ride with William on the mower or bull rake, depending on what he was doing. The hay, once cut, dried and raked, was stacked with the help of swinging boom stackers, moved from stack to stack as needed. Once a stack was finished, those on top who had helped to place and level the hay coming up would ride to the ground again on a sling. When William was working on the stackers, he'd allow the children up to the top of the stack to help, and then they'd ride down on the sling, shrieking with excitement as the sling dangled and swung. At night, the men would wash in the creek and sleep early, after a game or two of poker or horseshoes on the shorn field, because the mornings began at four thirty; they could be heard talking quietly in their tents or else snoring. The Chinese cook smoked in the evenings outside his cabin, the fumes of opium and the joss he burned inside hanging over the clean scent of hay like an exotic curtain. Margaret rose early to help catch and harness the horses. She loved the sight of them in the dawn field, standing in groups near a cottonwood, and their movement toward her as she rattled oats in a bucket to catch their attention, looming out of the mist, huge and sombre. She had her favourites among the working teams — a pair of Clydesdales named Bill and Florrie, who had massive feet and densely feathered fetlocks. She liked to fit their harnesses on while they held their big heads low for her, and they always stood stock still while she fastened the straps under their bellies and tails. In the mornings their cool faces smelled of grass, an occasional seed caught in the fine hairs on their lips. The way they wrinkled their lips around their teeth reminded her of the toothless old men she saw in church, working their gums while the minister preached of God and angels.

Hay camp was a pleasant diversion from Margaret's preoccupation with Nicholas. Up on the hay meadows, she stopped half-expecting to see him riding up to the house, she wasn't reminded of his mouth as he kissed her under the trees on the road to Douglas Lake, and she had no privacy in the tent she shared with her sisters to fill with the memory of dancing with him in the Nicola Hall, the pressure of his hand on the small of her back. When she did remember, it was the weight of his body against hers during a waltz, his face against her hair. It was kissing him while around them lightning crackled and snapped, the taste of his mouth. She remembered the shock and excitement in his eyes as the two of them steadied Thistle while the stallion grunted and thrust into her, his teeth bared as he released his seed into her damp mysterious body. And Margaret remembered washing herself by lamplight that evening, and how she had felt she was drowning in pleasure.

The days at the hay camp were sunny and warm, an occasional afternoon storm coming in from the northeast to cloud the skies, produce thunderheads and summer lightning, then pass as quickly as it arrived. When the hay was all stacked and the family had packed up their belongings, the wagon returned them to the home ranch, where the garden was flourishing and the red-tailed hawk chicks in the big cottonwood were beginning to fly, their parents teaching them tricks of aviation and pursuit. The songbirds were fledging, too, just in time for the parent hawks to teach their young to hunt inexperienced larks, as well as ground squirrels and the marmots whistling on the rough shoulders of the erratics.

There was a letter from Nicholas to say he was coming to Spahomin for four days in early August. Before he arrived, Margaret rode to her grandmother's cabin to help her gather rose hips for drying. She tried to time her visits with a plant trip so that she could learn how and where to gather the roots, stems, and berries that her grandmother used for food and medicine. It was one thing to sit in the kitchen and hear Grandmother Jackson describe how to dig up a tuber or remove a certain portion of a tree's bark and another to walk the dry hills or creek banks with the gathering baskets and watch exactly how much bark to take or whether the berries were at the right point of ripeness. The rose hips were perfect, plump and full. They filled one basket, and then Grandmother carefully cut some stems of the rose bushes to take back to use for basket handles. They found some tall mint growing on the banks of a creek and cut many stems of it to dry for keeping bugs away from the beds.

"I'll put some of this inside the pillows," said Grandmother Jackson. "The feathers get musty, and the mint will make them fresh."

"Nicholas has written me to say he's coming in a few days. Do you mind him staying with you?" Margaret wanted to hear her grandmother's opinion of the man whose name filled her with such pleasure.

"He is a nice young man, and I enjoy his company. So many of our young men are anxious to be accepted by the white people, and they haven't the time to listen to the old stories. Some don't even want the language any longer. In my heart, this is part of my fear, the old fear that we will disappear. If we don't speak our language, tell our stories, feed and heal our bodies with what the Creator has put on our doorsteps, then who will we be? Who? It is very good to have someone come who thinks the stories are important. Your mother says he came to look for you the last time he was in the valley and was disappointed not to find you. This time he will be luckier, I think."

They laid out the rose hips in single layers in shallow baskets when they returned to the cabin, and peeled the stems of rose wood and laid them out along the rafters to dry. Then the two women prepared a meal of bacon and bannock and took it out onto the porch to eat with mugs of strong tea. Margaret had promised to milk her family's cow that evening, so she left and rode towards home on a trail that the Reserve cattle used, leading along the river where it left the road. She was about half-way home when Daisy snorted and balked, reluctant to go further. And Margaret could see why: just ahead, standing ankle deep in the river, was a big black bear, her two cubs just behind her. Although Daisy had squealed before Margaret could pat her neck and direct her, the bear was busy at the river's edge and hadn't yet got wind of them.

Keeping a tight rein, Margaret backed Daisy along the trail to where a cluster of young willows sheltered the water. She could see that the bear had a fish, a salmon, and was tearing open its belly; the eggs shone in the body cavity and the cubs were being encouraged to take a mouthful. The sharp stink of bear stung Margaret's nostrils and Daisy's, as well. She was beginning to fret on the short rein, skittering and blowing. The sow turned and saw them there among the willows and dropped the fish. Clacking her teeth, she started toward them, then retreated, growling and snapping. The river was too fast for Margaret to attempt to cross it with Daisy in such an agitated state, and the rise on the other side of the trail was too steep to take at a run. She did not want to turn and retreat and risk having the bear catch up with them. Although bears looked clumsy and slow, Margaret knew how fast they could run, especially when provoked.

The sow bear turned to her cubs and grunted a command. Before Margaret could think, the little family was swiftly climbing the steep grassy slope across the trail and vanishing over the hill. Margaret was so relieved to see them go that she collapsed over Daisy's neck, exhaling the breath she had not been aware she was holding.

Returning to the ranch was anticlimactic. Frightened as she had been, recognizing the danger of the situation, Margaret was thrilled to see the bear and her young at the river, eating the rosy salmon flesh and then disappearing into the landscape so quickly. There was such beauty in their glossy coats, their long claws, the glistening eggs in the belly of the fish. Her father was up with the cattle, and she told her mother instead, expecting it would worry her but needing to share the story.

Instead, Jenny told her, "The black bear was my father's guardian spirit, you know. I always liked bears and was never afraid of them when we picked berries or put our weirs across the river. My father said they could hear what you said about them. You should never say hurtful things because then they wouldn't come when you needed them. And we did need them sometimes, for their fat and their meat, and for winter robes."

Margaret was surprised to hear her mother talk of such things. Because she had not undertaken a puberty ceremony and because she seldom spoke of her childhood, her daughter supposed that she wasn't interested in the old ways. She asked her mother about her grandmother's guardian spirit.

"It's the mountain goat," Jenny said. "We don't see them here, but she was from Shulus, you know, and there were some over there. It suits her, she was always scrambling about on the mountainsides looking for plants. But if I'd had a guardian, I'd have wanted it to be the bear because it was special to my father. Now, do you want your supper before you milk the cow or after?"

Margaret took her time with the milking as she thought about her mother. Because she didn't talk much about her life before William, it was easy to forget she'd had one. She was the daughter who had been lost to the priests; that was the way Grandmother Jackson seemed to think of her. Yet they were not estranged, nothing so dramatic. Jenny still visited her mother at Spahomin from time to time, though she was closer to her brother and sister; and she always sent little gifts to her mother when Margaret went over alone. But from what she'd just said, she *had* felt a bond with her father. He'd been dead for years, having been taken by consumption when Margaret was a tiny child. She had one memory of him: sitting in the cabin Grandmother lived in, hearing him tell a story about Old-one creating the Nicola Valley and making the mountains and the original people. At home she had been hearing about God and the garden of Eden from her mother and father; she thought Eden must look like Culloden, all golden grass, ringed with ponderosas, and God like her grandfather, whom she thought of as the Old-one. She had not doubted that he could do anything he put his mind to, his voice was that deep and strong as he told the story, and she didn't notice how thin he was, how wasted his arms, and how he kept coughing into a bloody handkerchief.

Margaret dreamed of the bears that night, the surprise of the mother as she heard Daisy's snorting and caught the scent of them in the air, and she heard again the snapping of her teeth. In the dream she dismounted and went down to the river to greet them, then ran with them up the steep hill, her loose black coat hanging from her bones. In her mouth, the taste of fish eggs and raw flesh, and the husks of rose hips flecking the dung she left in the excitement of their departure. How will I tell my parents I've left them, she wondered, will I still have speech? But when she tried to talk, only muffled grunts came from her mouth, her tongue a thick obstacle, immovable. When she woke, she found three black hairs on her pillow, too coarse to have come from her own head.

Nicholas came with a little gift, a photograph he'd taken of Margaret's favourite from among her grandmother's baskets — the split cedar with the pattern of deer hoof and entrails. It was sitting on the sinew chair on the porch, weathered railings to one side.

"I didn't know you had a camera!" she said. "Did you take many photographs?"

"I'm still learning how to use it," he confessed, "and quite a lot of them didn't turn out. I tried taking the glass plates away to develop, and some of them fogged or the emulsion cracked. I want to make a record of things, though, and your grandmother's baskets are exquisite. I thought that from the beginning, but I can verify it now that I've spent time looking at others and consulting with Dr. Newcombe. He has given me instructions to photograph everything. Perhaps you could help me with the equipment if you're interested."

When Margaret had been younger, a Dr. Sutton had practised medicine in Nicola. He'd come to the ranch to attend to a cowhand who'd broken an arm, and he was often seen at the socials. He was a big man and hard of hearing, the result of a childhood bout of scarlet fever. But he claimed the bracing air of the valley was bringing his hearing back. His interests had included photography, and he was the one whom William had traded the quarter side of beef for a family portrait to send to Astoria. Dr. Sutton had photographed his servant as well as other people in the valley; it was a point of pride to have been taken by the doctor.

"Your grandmother is letting me use the old smokehouse as

a darkroom. That'll be perfect for the images of her baskets and everything nearby. I've got a tent, too, to take up for shots of more remote areas like that old campsite your father showed me. And I'd like to take some shots of the kikuli houses down by the lake, maybe with some other things to make them look as though they're still in use. I know people haven't lived in them for twenty years or so, but they're still part of active memory, your grandmother's memory."

Margaret examined the equipment Nicholas pulled out of his bags. Glass plates wrapped in canvas, jars of solutions, pans, a bundle that proved to be the windowless tent to use as a portable darkroom. Nicholas explained that he didn't really need the darkroom now that he'd been given plates coated with gelatin emulsion — before coming to the valley, he'd used collodion plates, which needed to be developed immediately — but he wanted to develop the plates anyway to make sure he'd got the images he wanted.

"How stupid I'd feel if I took them back to Spences Bridge or shipped them to Victoria and then discovered I had nothing at all to show for my work. So I'll develop them here and make contact prints. I'll teach you everything I know if you like, but I'm really still learning, too."

I've seen the photographs taken in the early years of the century and have looked deeply into their images to find a clue about the lives there. They hover and circle, sometimes surfacing in sleep with a clarity never experienced in dreams, as if they are memories of my own. The mule-drawn wagons on the Cariboo road. The astonishing prospect of Hell's Gate on the Fraser River, racks of salmon drying on the rocks beside the chasm. Views of the stopping houses with plumes of smoke rising from their chimneys, women in long dresses drying their hands on aprons as they greeted the travellers. The crowded courtroom in

Kamloops, Bill Miner with a bemused look on his face as he rested his chin in his hand in the prisoners box. In the early pictures of men at work, the loggers pose on their springboards, one at each end of a gut fiddle, ready to topple the immense trees of our beginnings. Doukhobor women draw the ploughs over plains of unbroken grass in pairs, straining to the task. And there are the photographs of the valley itself, a kikuli house, c.1898, with the ladder showing at the opening but otherwise abandoned, Dr. Sutton's picture of a woman net-fishing the Nicola River in 1900, the Roi.pellst family in 1914, posed in front of a tule shelter, their buckskin clothing so finely worked and regal, so palpable that I want to straighten the fringe with my fingers. I know that they wouldn't have worn those clothes regularly in 1914 because I've seen the other photographs, too — Frederick Dally's shot of people praying at Lytton, Dr. Sutton's photo of a mealtime in 1898, tents of canvas, most people with their backs to the camera, one fellow standing with his hands behind his back, his suspenders holding up his worsted trousers. I want to enter the photograph, walk into the camp from the aspens to the left, be given a tin plate of bannock and a piece of fish. The grass is dry and heavy with seeds. I could take these seeds forward with me, hidden in my clothing, my hair, an amulet to summon the past into my life, extant, viable as lupin seeds removed from the stomach of a mastodon, to germinate and flourish in the soil of the present.

Nicholas had persuaded members of the Jackson family to allow him to photograph them in traditional clothing in front of a tule house that he and August's boys had reconstructed. Grandmother Jackson had tule mats stored in her cabin and drew sketches for them to show the way the poles were placed, the mats layered and fastened. Inside the house was airy and smelled of dry grass. Nicholas was so fond of its interior that he decided to sleep in it for the remainder of his visit. He'd lie in the silver latticed screen the moonlight made on the ground as it filtered through the spots in the mats where the stalks of dried bulrush held together with Indian hemp had separated slightly. He'd look up towards the smoke-hole and imagine summer villages of these shelters, the smell of curing fish and bear fat in the air, baskets of drying berries, and fish nets spread out for mending on the bushes. He wanted to dream his way back into that life, become a part of it, however temporarily, and carry away the smoke in his clothing, the foxtail barley seeds in his hair. He couldn't explain why he found it so fascinating, even haunting, why he wanted to enter it in the enigmatic realm of dream, knowing any other way was impossible. But when he slept and dreamed, it was of his father in the Ausable River, casting a line with a mayfly fashioned of coloured thread and feather on its end, bracing himself against the strong current, his old creel over his shoulder. Or else he dreamed of his grandmother in Chantilly, brushing crumbs from her dining table with a little silver brush and pan, singing as she worked a fragment of Purcell's *Dido*.

Margaret helped with the shoot of the family standing by the tule lodge. They were wearing clothing of light buckskin and sage bark, elaborately ornamented with quillwork, painted designs, beadwork and dentalia. Some of the old clothing, saved and wrapped in the burlap bags that potatoes were stored in, was still used for ceremonial purposes, but other pieces had been begged, borrowed and stolen for museum collections, some even purchased, a fair price arrived at and agreed upon. August and Alice stood side by side, looking solemn, and three of their children gathered around them. August wore his father's headband of coyote tails and carried his hammerstone carved with the head and claws of a bear. The smallest child, Tessie, wore a headband decorated with buttons. Margaret thought they looked wonderful, so stately and serious, transformed almost into the shadowy figures of the ancestors who were spoken of so often and who had worn these clothes as naturally as their own skins. She had the sense again of being in two worlds at once, wanting one so intensely that she felt her heart might break but knowing, too, that it was not her complete home, the one which involved meals at the long table in her father's house, sewing by lamplight as Aunt Elizabeth and Grandmother Stuart had shown her, cross-stitching and delicate French knots articulating a verse on fine linen with borders of bluebells and purple English violets while her father played sweet airs on his violin. She travelled out from this home to hear the glorious voice of Canada's Queen of Song, knew every inch of the fields and creeks of the ranch, played chess on the long winter evenings with her father under the low window looking out to stars and the occasional owl alighting in the bare cottonwoods. But a part of her, too, walked on the dry grass of Spahomin, knew where to find lilies, where to find wild potatoes to bring back to her grandmother's cabin. Walking that land, with her favourite basket over her shoulder, she could hear the voices of the dead rattling like dry seedpods in the wind. Grandmother Jackson said that sometimes the dead longed for the living so deeply that they followed them through their days, touching a beloved's shoulder as lightly as a moth might so that the person would turn to see who was so close. At night they might stand by the bed of a dreamer and breathe memories into an open sleeping mouth. Or you could feel a hand fit itself into your own, dry as dust and light, oh, very light, never a burden if the dead ones chose to sit behind you on the horse or to share your bed.

After he had the composition he wanted, Nicholas asked the Jackson family to remain where they stood so that he could show Margaret how to use the camera. She stepped up to the tripod and put her eye to the viewfinder while Nicholas arranged the hood of dark cloth over her head. She could smell the varnished wood casing of the camera and the acrid chemical as Nicholas slid a plate into place.

"You should see them here as you would like the photograph

to look. Think of balance and frame. The light is good, and we've got the magnesium to improve it. When you're ready, we'll take the shot."

Margaret looked through the arrangement of glass and mirrors, expecting to see her family members in their unfamiliar clothing against the shelter of dried tule-grass. That was what she looked for. But instead she felt light-headed, goosebumps on her arms and shoulders made her shiver, and she could feel the little hairs on the back of her neck rise, one by one. What she could see through the viewfinder was a group of people moving through the grass, one of them putting an armload of sticks by the fire, a few children, so airy she could almost see through them, and some thin horses in the distance. Although the day was still, she could hear something, a wind, voices, almost whispers. She reached one hand toward them but it was as though she didn't exist: the figures spoke quietly to one another, thrust sticks into the fire, turned a mat that was lying over a wild rose bush. One of the children coughed, one of the adult figures looked worried at the harsh phlegmy sound. Another child played in the grass with a few small stones, humming. The sound was like bees in flowers. When Nicholas asked quietly if she was ready, Margaret nodded under the cloth and the ribbon of magnesium snapped and burned. What she had seen was gone, and it was Aunt Alice and Uncle August smiling at her, a little self-conscious in their buckskin.

Nicholas inserted another plate and replaced the hood over Margaret's head. She closed her eyes hard before opening them again to look through the viewfinder. With a hand, she gestured to Tessie to turn her face to profile, she gestured to August to straighten the hammerstone. They moved together a little as she indicated and then held the pose until she had taken the shot she wanted.

She blinked in the sunlight and shuddered. Nicholas took the glass plates to the smokehouse to begin the process of developing, and she followed him, told him what she'd seen, hesitating at what she might call the diaphanous figures she'd seen through the viewfinder.

"It wasn't them at all, it was something else entirely. Yet someone still of this place. Like a dream, as though I was dreaming. I could almost see through the shapes of the children. Do you remember I told you about seeing the men being taken to Kamloops in the rain for the train robbery trial? It was that kind of seeing."

Nicholas looked at her, puzzled. "I don't know what to say. Perhaps the lens or plates are fogging, but wouldn't I have noticed that? When I looked through the viewfinder, I saw them perfectly clearly, August and Alice, I mean. But we'll develop these and see what turns up. Do you feel ill or feverish? It's very hot today, and maybe you've had too much sun."

"No, nothing like that. You forget I'm used to this heat, I've never known any other kind of summer. But I hope I haven't ruined the shot. Maybe I'll feel better in a shady place." But saying that, she knew it wasn't the sun that had caused her to hear the humming of that child, to see the sticks thrust into the fire.

When the plates were developed, Nicholas began to see how good the photographs would be. When he had time, he'd make contact prints from the plates. August's family looked magnificent in the dry air, and the light had been perfect, helped only a little by magnesium. Nicholas could see on the negative plate that each element was recorded with a clarity he hadn't yet achieved with his photographs.

By the next evening, Nicholas had a group of photographs drying on a wire he'd strung from the ceiling of the temporary darkroom. The pungency of his chemicals was almost overwhelming, and he caught whiffs of smoked fish from the oils that had penetrated the wooden walls over the years. The shots that Margaret took were the best. He couldn't say why, but the people in front of the tule lodge were so alive and potent in the clothing of their forefathers and mothers. They shimmered in the clear summer air, strangely lit as though by fire. Margaret, who had been working alongside him, was quiet as she watched the images come forward on the paper, watched as he toned with gold chloride, washed, fixed, and puzzled over each photograph.

Nicholas turned to Margaret. "You see how different your shots are from mine? I swear we looked at the same scene, but you've made something of it that I wasn't able to. Do you see what I mean? Yours are, well, they're alive somehow. You've made a connection, like eye contact or something, I don't know what to call it."

The girl nodded. "Yes, I can see the difference. I had a feeling they'd be good when we made the exposure. I can't tell you how, I just did. But it isn't quite what I saw, you know, or at least the first shot isn't. You thought the plates might be fogging, but it's clear they weren't. When I looked through the viewfinder that first time, I saw people moving, doing things with a fire. I heard a child cough, heard another child humming as he played on the ground. It was my uncle's family and yet it wasn't, quite. I've had this feeling before about other things — once when I was gathering plants with my grandmother, for instance, and then the train robbers. It's a little frightening, but I would like to try some more, if you're willing."

Margaret and Nicholas rode home to the ranch side by side that evening, holding hands and talking of an expedition to the kikuli site by the lake in the next few days. It was so clear that they could see the mountains beyond Nicola Lake turning crimson as the sun went down. A sparrow hawk was hunting for grasshoppers and field mice over the pasture before the ranch, and they stopped to watch it hover and plunge, sounding its shrill killy-killy cry in the falling light. Ahead they could see the ranch in its grove of cottonwoods, two horses in the corral watching their progress, and then, one by one, the windows glowed as the lamps were lit by someone within. A ranch dog had spotted them coming and was barking on the edge of the road leading to the house.

"Will you come in for a meal?" Margaret asked.

"No, I'd better head back now while there's still some light." Pulling on her hand, Nicholas drew Margaret toward him until he could touch her face and kiss her. Her mouth was dusty and her hair smelled of the darkroom. They kissed until the dog trotted up to see what was taking the horses so long to arrive.

"Here's my escort to see me home," laughed Margaret, and then leaned to kiss Nicholas once more, releasing her reins in her attempt to get as close to him as she could. She wanted his smell on her hands and shoulders, the warmth of his breath on her neck. Her horse, impatient, started toward the barn, and she hastily reached down its neck for the reins, calling goodbye as she left.

Lying in her bed that night, Margaret recalled how she had felt after the Albani concert in May. She remembered sitting in the carriage with her face against the cool glass of the windows, wondering about her future. She had been amazed by Madame Albani, her singing and her gracious manner at the Slavin house. But she had been particularly taken by the younger singer, Eva Gautier, that evening, impressed that someone so young could have been so sure of herself to have made a career of singing. That evening, Margaret had tried to assess her own accomplishments, and they had been such modest ones — training horses, tracking coyotes across the grass, helping her grandmother dig up roots of blue camas. But now she felt she had discovered the thing she could direct her abilities toward: making photographs and recording the life of her valley. She had experienced the camera, its wood, the texture of the brass fittings and the gauges, the rack and pinion arrangement that adjusted the focus. Although she had been unnerved by the sight of the moving figures through the viewfinder, she had also known in a way beyond words that her images would be good ones. The process of developing and printing she was confident she could learn. All spring she'd had the feeling she was on a threshold. A darkened doorway led to her future, and she had not yet had the courage to even consider peering into its shadows. But now she knew she was ready to take the step across, to what and where, she was still uncertain, but she was filled with the sense of possibility. She had the map and now needed to learn to read its legend. And she had hope, hope that her family would permit her to do what she needed to do to learn more about photography, and hope that whatever she did, Nicholas would somehow be a part of it.

A receipt for a camera, purchased September, 1906, from Mary Spencer in Kamloops, accompanied by a letter.

Dear Miss Stuart,

Your father asked me to recommend a camera
for you. There are as many cameras as there are
photographers, but from his descriptions of your
interests, I am hopeful that you will enjoy this fine
Sanderson field camera as much as I did. I bought it
new, on a trip to London, in 1895. I must say I fell in
love with its appearance as much as anything. The
mahogany is such a pretty wood and the brass fittings
lovely, I think. The lens is a Beck Symmetrical, iris to
f64. If you ever have questions about it, please do write
to me. The reason I am willing to sell it is that it
simply hasn't been used for its true purpose, which is
field work, vast landscapes, skies. Increasingly my work
has been portraiture, weddings and civic events, and
I seldom work outdoors as I once did.

You will notice that the plate on the camera says
"G. Houghton, Son." This is the manufacturer. I was so
impatient to take possession of this camera that I went
directly to Mr. Houghton in High Holborn in order to

see the final stages of the camera's construction rather than wait for it at the dealer.

I had the outfit case modified by a local harness maker so that I could carry it on my back; that is what the straps are for. I had them made to be adjustable, and therefore the case is comfortable to wear over summer clothing or heavier winter wear.

This camera should be used, it should do what it does best, and I know you will employ it. I am gratified to hear of a young woman taking up this excellent calling. Please let me know how you progress, and best of luck to you.

I remain,
Sincerely yours,
Mary Spencer

The receipt acknowledges gratefully the sum of thirteen dollars and notes the inclusion of some eight-by-ten plates with the camera and its case.

Of course I wish the camera were available to look at, and I wonder where it might be found, if anywhere. If the hands of women are present in the textiles they have worked, the smoothing of their fingers imprinted in the furrows of quilted cotton and the tiny mice-feet of feather-stitching, in the sayings they have chosen to replicate on linen, then what remains of a woman in the camera she has used to frame her world? The apparitions of all the images she has sought and made visible on paper, would they linger in the workings of the camera, its polished mahogany body? I think of it as a repository for her soul, or part of her soul, everything her eager heart made a connection with by focusing and developing.

Chapter Ten

A TABLE COVER HAS ARRIVED, a cloth of yellowed damask, chewed in one corner by rats. The owner knew it was rats and not mice because she'd caught them at it in her storage room. The cloth had been a wedding gift to her mother in Bukovina in what was then the Austro-Hungarian Empire and had been brought to the prairies to a sod house on a windswept plain, dried buffalo bones and dung piled by the door. She wept when she learned she must use that as fuel. Hers was the experience of the young country, immigration, hardship, sorrow as one baby after another succumbed to whooping cough or scarlet fever. But the land was broken, as her husband had promised it would be, and lilacs were planted, wheat grown, children borne who lived and thrived, and those children went out into the world to do and become things undreamed of by their parents. This daughter had nursed in the old Mission Hospital in our community, married a fisherman and raised seven children of her own. She remembered the long winter nights on the prairie, tallow candles and then oil lamps illuminating the dark rooms, meals of turnips and salt pork, but every Sunday the table laid with the damask cloth, salt rubbed into any grease marks that dared to appear on it, and on Monday, which was wash day, the sight of it draped over a wolf willow to dry. It had been her own habit to use it on Sundays, too, until her children had all left home. She had put it in her storage room for mending one winter, kept being sidetracked by one thing after another, and then discovered it had been chewed by the rats that were a part of coastal life, living as she did in a house built right over the bay, its front part on footings that rocked slightly in storms when the tides buffeted them. I wrote her story down on a card and then gave her some information on the treatment of heirloom textiles. So much of the research discourages the use of these textiles as the practical objects most of them were intended to be. Light can fade, ultraviolet light can damage fibres, moist air and warmth encourage molds that stain fibres and cause deterioration. Folding and creasing cause streaking and fading and can cut threads. Yet many families love to use the things their grandmothers stitched or wove or quilted to keep a daily connection with their history. And most households don't rise to acid-free boxes and tissue. I suggest to this woman that we wash the cloth together after we vacuum it with low suction and then carefully dry it. And washing the damask cloth, our hands touching in the cool water, we are sharing the ceremony of Sunday meals in the sod house, passing bread across its white expanse in the ill-lit room, we are folding it, one at each end, after it has dried in the wind, and pressing it with sad-irons and steam flicked from an expert finger, and carefully putting it in a drawer to wait until the next Sunday meal. I tell her my own grandmother, for whom I am named Anna, brought such a table-cloth from her birthplace in Poland, and that it was used by my family for years until it finally wore away to a shred. After the exhibition, she has agreed to wrap her cloth in unbleached muslin and store it in a cedar-lined trunk. I'll give her a small sachet of dried lavender when the time comes.

1.
Margaret didn't sleep all night but kept going over in her mind the steps she needed to follow, rereading the owner's manual that had come with her new camera. At dawn she had been in the field for an hour, working out positions for the best light, preparing the plates,

climbing into the lower limbs of the cottonwood tree to secure the buckskin laces of the cradleboard in such a way that they could be seen through the viewfinder. The handle of the cradle was a length of wild rose cane, stripped and polished by years of handling. Margaret had borrowed the cradleboard from a family at Spahomin who had used it for each of their six children, the old custom of abandoning the device after a child had outgrown it no longer prevalent. When she was ready to take the shot, she noticed that the roan gelding had wandered into her field of vision, attracted by the first rays of sun. Her first instinct was to include him in the shot, and then, after exposing the first plate, she chased him away to try another shot without him.

CRADLEBOARD IN A TREE, August, 1906.
(gelatin-silver print)

Taken at sunrise at the western edge of Culloden pasture. A cradleboard with the buckskin laces dangling is hanging from a young cottonwood tree. A grey horse is just to the right of the tree, head down as though sleeping. The soft light filtering through the cottonwood branches gives the photograph an atmosphere reminiscent of the platinotypes made by Clarence H. White in the late 1800s.

2.
She hadn't planned the next shot but had been returning on Daisy from another shoot with all her equipment and had come upon the place where she'd found the drinking tube the previous year. It was late afternoon, with clusters of high cloud in the sky. The

sun was just passing through one such cluster, creating
an ethereal light. Margaret hurriedly got out her
camera and took three shots. The third included some
things she was taking home to use as props — an old
pair of her grandfather's moccasins, a necklace, a few
of Uncle August's old tools. As she looked through
the viewfinder, she felt the sensation again of seeing
presences. This time, a girl came from nowhere to place
a small figure of an animal fashioned out of wisps of
grass and a little clump of brown-eyed Susans among
the rocks. Her face was painted with a wide yellow
band across the forehead. Margaret remembered her
grandmother saying that this represented the grey trail
or the Milky Way. Was this girl the dead girl? And was
this like a dream, seeing her through the viewfinder?
There were stories about those who dreamed of the
dead, their heads touching the pillows of the dead,
stories of the dead returning to wear the clothing of
the living. Painting your face or purifying your body
with a sweatbath could take away the events promised
by the dreams. Taking her eye from the camera to look,
Margaret saw only the boulders, irradiated by the
aureole of the sun behind clouds. She quickly took
the props from her saddlebag and placed them by the
boulder she'd seen the girl approach with her offerings.

GRAVE-SITE ABOVE LAUDER CREEK, August 1906.
GELATIN-SILVER PRINT

In the foreground, boulders heaped in an informal cairn
with assorted boulders strewn around the central
grouping. Tall stalks of grass cast a netting of shadows
over the ground. Beyond, a grove of trees, their
shadows clean shapes that echo the dark lines of grass.
A shaft of intense light coming from behind high cloud

bisects the photograph, illuminating the central cairn. A few artifacts — a necklace of animal teeth, a stone hammer with an image carved into its head, a pair of moccasins — lie to one side of the largest boulder, as if abandoned.

3.

"Will you go with me to the kikuli site? I thought I'd ask Tessie and Jack to come along in case I want to use people in some of the shots. If we go early, we can take a picnic and even swim. Nicola Lake never gets very warm, but if the day is hot, we'll be glad to have it for cooling off."

KIKULI HOUSES BY NICOLA LAKE, August, 1906.
GELATIN-SILVER PRINT

Three winter houses near the lakeshore, the notched poles that served as ladders protruding from the west side of the entrance holes on two of them, the third pole in the foreground of the photograph. Clumps of bunchgrass growing on the earth covering the framework indicate that these are not recent structures. Two children stand to the far left of the photograph, each dressed in leggings and a buckskin shirt, some ornamentation woven into the fringe of the shirts. The children are carrying lidded baskets of the sort used as kettles.

4.

Wanting to capture something of what she'd seen at the hay camp earlier in the summer, Margaret planned two shoots in a row to take advantage of the fact that the Indians were taking a second cutting of hay off the Reserve's fields. She slept at her grandmother's cabin and was awake at four in order to replicate the image she'd loved of the work horses materializing out of the mist near the creek to be harnessed for the day. She tried a number of shots of the rakes and stackers, the men in their work clothes, a group of children coming across the field with baskets of food and bottles of water, the teams of horses waiting out the worst of the heat under a grove of aspens, and a close-up shot of a large cluster of thistles gone to seed.

HORSES AT DAWN, September, 1906.
GELATIN-SILVER PRINT

Two massive horses, Clydesdales (as evidenced by their blazes, each with four white stockings and heavily feathered fetlocks), are emerging out of a misty field. A fence of grey boards bisects the photograph horizontally to the right of the horses. A grove of trees balances the composition to the left of the horses.

HAYFIELD AT SPAHOMIN RESERVE,
September, 1906.
GELATIN-SILVER PRINT

An expanse of shorn grass, articulated by high mounds of hay, one of them with a boom stacker positioned over it. Two teams of horses with flat wagons behind them are visible at the far end of the field. The light is clear, and the shadows cast by the stacker timbers indicate that it is around noon.

5.

The baskets gave her the most trouble because she had in mind that she wanted to photograph them individually, to take their portraits, and it was difficult to arrange the compositions so that the imbrications achieved the clarity she felt they deserved. In the end, after a number of attempts to place the baskets in settings that told something of their making — among piles of dried rushes, lengths of cedar roots, heaps of various barks — she settled on simply shooting each basket from an angle that gave it a clean shadow.

A SERIES OF SIX BASKETS FROM THE NICOLA VALLEY, September, 1906.
GELATIN-SILVER PRINT

Each basket is photographed on a flat rock surrounded by pasture. Two are of coiled cedar-root, two are open-work, of twigs, and two are of laced bark, birch or poplar, and these are decorated with painted designs. A note on the back of the photo of one bark basket says that the pigments were made of iron pyrites, lichens, copper salts and animal grease. One of the cedar-root baskets is decorated with a fine design, geometric in nature, noted on the back as "deer hoof and entrail." The other cedar-root basket is a fly pattern of different shadings and has a lid hinged with buckskin. The open-work baskets are particularly beautiful. Each photograph is well composed, but two suffer from light leaks around the edges.

6.

"I haven't been here since the day of the capture. This is where I tied my horse after I saw the wisp of smoke coming up from over the little knoll and all the men sneaking up to it. And right there, that's where Mr. Edwards and his friends were sitting. They had a skillet over the flames and a coffee pot on that flat rock there. That man who was shot, Shorty Dunn, he ran over there first, and that's when the shooting began. We could probably find bullets lodged in some of the aspens if we looked. And over here, where the marsh begins, is where the cranes usually nest, the reason I'd come here in the first place. How still it is! All you can hear are the ducks muttering in Chapperon Lake."

THE ROBBER'S GLEN, September, 1906.
GELATIN-SILVER PRINT

An area of aspen trees on a slope of ground leading to some rushes and reeds on the edge of a body of water. The trees make strong vertical lines across the entire width of the photograph. In the foreground, to the left, is a small ring of stones describing a fireplace, partly covered in leaf litter. Shafts of sunlight filter down through the tree-tops.

7.

Because she knew the photograph of August and his family standing in traditional clothing by the tule shelter told only part of the story of their lives in particular and Reserve life in general, Margaret took shots of their cabin, inside and out, and a variety of scenes about Spahomin.

ALICE'S WASH DAY, September, 1906.
GELATIN-SILVER PRINT

A woman in a plain dress with a bandana tied around her head is doing her family's laundry in a creek. A pile of clothing is on one side of her as she squats beside the creek, scrubbing a pair of men's trousers against a river rock. A number of items are spread over the bushes to dry — bed-sheets, a child's dress, several shirts, a pair of bloomers. The woman's face is turned toward the camera, the shadow of a smile on her mouth.

8.
Margaret spent several days persuading her grandmother to let her take a portrait shot. When the old lady finally agreed, Margaret brought the sinew chair out onto the porch of the cabin. Asking her grandmother to sit in the chair, she set up the camera and tried various angles before she found the one she wanted.

MRS. SUSANNAH JACKSON AT HOME, SPAHOMIN. September, 1906.
GELATIN-SILVER PRINT

An elderly woman, seated on a chair on a weathered wooden porch, looking straight at the viewer. The chair has thrown a shadow of fine fretwork onto the wall behind it, where animal skins are stretched as though to dry. The woman is wearing a calico dress, bare legs, a pair of moccasins. Her own shadow appears behind her, almost exactly fitting the outline of her form on the chair. She is holding a nosegay of flowers, and on her left wrist can be seen what appears to be a tattoo.

Nicholas was packaging Margaret's photographs into a special portfolio to send to Dr. Boas. He thought they were extremely fine, and he wanted his mentor to see them.

"He's very interested in photography itself, and not just as a way of recording anthropology research. He often recommends exhibits for us to see. I remember one in particular, the work of a man named Adam Vroman, who spent a number of years making photographs of the Indians of the pueblos. His portraits are magnificent. Another man, O'Sullivan, he'd photographed some of the terrible battles of the Civil War, Gettysburg, Bull Run, the Slaughter Pen at Round Top, and others as well. Later he went west with geographical survey teams. His pictures of the ruined village sites near the Grand Canyon are extraordinary. And there's a beauty I remember, one of a cliff house at Canyon de Chelly. You can see the striations of the rock, his focus is so clear."

The places sounded a haunted poetry to Margaret as she watched her photographs disappear into tissue and card. Canyon de Chelly, Bull Run . . . for a moment, she saw a grey field with some trees to the side and bodies lying side by side, like felled logs. Some were draped with striped blankets, looking sodden. She could smell stale gunpowder and the cloying odour of blood. When Grandmother Stuart had visited two years earlier, she and William sat one evening by a blazing fire of pine logs discussing the terrible war that had occurred in their country. William had been a boy in Astoria during the battles of the Civil War, but news of them had come across the land by newspaper and telegraph. His own father had been a supporter, in word at least, of the Union Army, and had been angry as the lists of the dead, published in the newspapers, grew longer and longer. William and his mother talked quietly of those days, and Margaret heard the names of the foreign cities softly punctuating their conversation: Petersburg, Richmond, and loveliest of all, Arlington, Virginia, a name like falling water. Now, remembering Arlington, she shuddered, associating it for reasons beyond her knowledge with loss, with the terrible ceremonies of the dead. Shaking her head to clear her sight, she began to make a list of the photographs she was sending. Although she had the plates still, she wanted to keep track of the prints.

I have dreamed of a girl.

In all weathers I've travelled up to stand on the high plateau, to look around me half in excitement, half in fear. Although I know enough of my family background to know that the Nicola Valley does not figure in my past, no relation farmed here, no great-ancestor walked across these wide grasslands trapping small animals and skinning them carefully, no one fished the lakes, no one drew a needle of porcupine quill under the surface of a child's skin, pulling a thread blackened with charcoal to mark her for life. Yet I am no less branded than the horses that come to the truck, the arrows and crosses of their belonging delicate scars that tie them forever to a patch of grass. Each time I come, I wonder what I will discover — a small wildflower unnoticed until now; the remains of a blackbird's nest; a shadow in a corner of the photographs taken of trees, buildings, views of the far-off hills. And the shadow might have been a girl, tracing the narrative of her own belonging, unaware of me waiting in the years to come to find her in the pollen, the seeds I bring unnoticed in my clothing, the clump of southernwood I dig up with a spoon to take home for a dry garden. Waiting on the side of the road below Hamilton Mountain, I almost see her on her bay mare, obscured by dust and the shadow of a cloud. When

I sleep, she enters my dreams quietly, leaving a fine mesh of memory threaded with the tiniest of keepsakes, the hollow at my ankle pierced with the sharp seeds of rye.

At the bottom of the box of memorabilia, something has slid between the flaps of cardboard. An envelope, powdery as moth wings, foxed like dried and fading blood, and inside, a piece of paper folded into squares. I know what I will find before I open it: the certificate telling of her death, influenza, 1908, before she has even turned twenty. The language of mortality is so formal. Schedule B — Deaths. Name and surname of deceased. Certified cause of death, and duration of illness. Religious Denomination. The careful lettering of her name, the duration, three weeks, her physician, Dr. Tuthill. And was there a moment when the hand paused before filling in Presbyterian, from her father's Scottish upbringing, did a heart remember a girl crouched in a sweat lodge, sweet juniper steaming on hot rocks? *How angels move.* Is it too much to imagine her still among the hills or seen in the cheekbones of a girl selling ice cream in Merritt, wiping tables at the Quilchena Hotel, leading a group of green riders across the rangeland at Douglas Lake?

After the photographs had gone to New York, Margaret was too busy to think about camera work. The ranch was gearing up for the fall cattle drive, and as usual she would accompany her father on the round-up and then to Kamloops to the buyers. They would take two full days and part of a third to make the trip, spending the first night near Stump Lake, where the cowhands and the Stuarts would sleep in an abandoned cabin and barn while the cattle rested and foraged on bunchgrass. The second night would be spent between Brigade Lake and Knutsford, depending on time and weather. They'd rise very early on the third morning and try to drive the cattle to the corrals by the railway station by mid-morning. Some years they would have trouble — a minor stampede when a grizzly met them on the trail, tearing the chest out of a steer before the cowboss shot him dead; some losses when a couple of young steers got into a patch of larkspur and ended up bloated on the ground, unable to continue; and once there was a sudden hard freeze-up at the higher elevation that upset the cattle and horses, coming as it did without warning.

Nicholas was working hard at his information-gathering, and there wasn't much time for long rides together on his irregular trips to the valley from his base at Spences Bridge. He wrote letters to Margaret, which she would take out to the creek, reading them under the cottonwoods which were beginning to lose their leaves.

I've been out to a series of deep pools near Spences Bridge where a few men were using bag nets of bark and twine. These were hung from hoops of fir with rings made of animal horn. They are very beautiful and work well, too. The feasts of salmon are wonderful, and everywhere you can smell the fish drying on racks in the sun. At first I found it almost nauseating, but now it is simply a note in the complex melody of the air. I was lucky enough to be asked to go night-fishing with a group of young men Charles Walkem introduced me to. They used torches of pitch-pine, and it was eerie to watch them spearing the fish from rock shelves along the river, like looking at old photographs. We went out in a canoe, too, and they speared from the sides of the boat. Some of the fish were enormous.

Margaret was familiar with these methods from her mother's family, although on the smaller creeks they usually used weirs. She had helped take fish that had been lured into traps within the weir systems, some of them speared and some of them raked in with gaffs. Her mother's brothers always brought a supply of fresh and dried fish to the Stuarts in exchange for beef or pork or young stock. She knew what Nicholas meant by the odour of drying fish. It was everywhere this time of year, hanging in the air near the drying racks and shifted about by wind. She thought of it as one of the smells of autumn, tied to the season like new hay to summer and fresh scallions to spring. Sometimes in winter she would pull an item of clothing, unworn since the fall, out of her wardrobe and be surprised at the faint smell of smoke and fish contained in its fibres.

The prospect of Nicholas leaving entirely caught Margaret unaware on a visit he made to the valley in early October. Walking in the field behind the home ranch, he told her he had nearly completed the work he had set out for himself upon arriving.

"I've made notes, made drawings, photographed everything and everyone, conducted many interviews, and I can't really put off going back to the university any longer. I still have course work to complete, and then I'll treat the translation as a thesis, perhaps writing a monograph of my own as a kind of appendix to Mr. Teit's work."

Margaret was quiet. She had not forgotten his other life, exactly, but in her pleasure at his company, the attraction she felt not just to him but to his ideas and work, she had put aside her knowledge that his time in the valley would end. She looked at him and touched his arm, not quite trusting her voice to say what she felt. He took her hand and they walked a little further.

"I have been thinking almost constantly of what I need to say to you, Margaret," Nicholas began, his own voice tentative. "You see, I could not have imagined, when I arrived here, how I would come to feel about you. Everything seemed so clear — I would gather my data, talk to people, make some contacts that might serve me over the years for future work in this area. I suppose I hoped to find the valley congenial, even to make a friend or two.

Those things are true beyond my dreams. But I had not counted on falling in love, though that is the most important thing of all. And am I right in thinking your feelings are the same?"

Margaret nodded, and for a few minutes they walked, the ranch buildings receding as they began to climb the eastern ridge above the field. The profession of love surprised her a little; she knew the current of emotion running between them was powerful, but she hadn't yet given it a name. She thought of it like water, sometimes fast moving as a spring freshet, sometimes more placid and quiet, like a pool. And, like water, mysterious and lovely.

"Nicholas, it's hard to talk about this, to find the right words, although I've thought it out in my own mind. Before you arrived, I really had not considered the future, my future, that is. The days passed happily enough, there were things to do, to look forward to, but no future, if you know what I mean. Then my father took us to Kamloops to hear Madame Albani sing, and I began to wonder about my life. There are girls who stay with their families all their lives, my Aunt Elizabeth did that, but I don't think it would be a good thing. We are isolated, as you know, and I wouldn't want to become one of those elderly spinsters, fearful of the world."

"You have a year or two to go before we can think of you as a spinster, and then some before you are elderly."

Margaret continued, "I have also begun to see a little how I am placed in the world and how it might affect my future. There is Spahomin and my relations, there is the ranch, and there is also Astoria. Aunt Elizabeth, who is certainly not fearful of the world, wrote earlier in the year to suggest that I might want to come to them for an extended stay, perhaps even travel to Europe with them. I kept thinking that I had to choose which family I belong to more."

"I hadn't thought of it like that, but yes, I can see your difficulty. You have a foot in two worlds, it seems, but I wonder if you must choose one or the other. Can you have both?"

Margaret felt grateful. "I'm beginning to understand that a choice would be impossible. My grandmother Jackson once told me that her people mourned the loss of their territory when the reserves were established, and it was more than the fact that they had lost land, because they didn't exactly think of the land as their possession. It was more that they knew who they were in relation to rocks and other places in the landscape, places that had meaning or where important things had happened. And not just in their own time but in memory. Well, I never knew the Nicola Valley before the reserves, of course, but I have never known any other place, either. Everything that ever happened to me has happened here. Each place on our ranch speaks to me, it has its own meaning or memory attached to it. The corral where I learned to ride, the cranes' marsh where I saw the train robbers. I have become acquainted with ancestors in the hills and pastures in a strange way. And this is the country where I met you, too. Yet I feel I must try to do something with my life that is mine. I was so happy when you taught me to use your camera and then when Father bought me my own because I thought it might be the thing I've been hoping for, without knowing what to expect. I would like to learn about photography, and I mean to now, so that I can make a record of the lives here, past and present."

Nicholas was watching her while she spoke, listening as she tried to explain something that was obviously still forming in her mind. "Shall we sit down here in the grass? I have a suggestion to make, and I'd rather not be panting while I talk. This ridge is steeper than I thought, but what a wonderful view!"

Looking down, they could see the ranch buildings and hear the voices of Margaret's sisters and brother at play. A line of immaculate laundry was strung between two cottonwoods, and the sheets billowed and danced in the wind like ghosts.

"I wonder if you would consider coming to New York for an extended visit. Dr. Boas telegraphed me to say that he thinks your photographs are splendid and that you would benefit from a course in data-collecting if you're serious about continuing with photography. The ethnology field he wants to develop is still brand new, and he needs people who have something to offer. From what you've said about making photographs, I think there would be a place for you. I know my family would welcome you to stay in our home, my mother in particular, because she's so grateful for everything your family has done for me. And I would love to show you the sights of New York and take you to concerts, though nothing will compare to the vitality of Jack Thynne's banjo or that Irish fellow's fiddle. What do you say? Please say you'll come, and then I'll begin to make arrangements. I must leave soon, sooner than you'd be able to, perhaps, but I'll find out about trains and anything else you'll need to know."

Margaret did not reply immediately but looked intently at the ranch below them, as if an answer might be found in the voices of the children or in the little herd of horses trotting across the corral to the summons of a bucket of oats. Magpies were hanging around the corral, loud in their observations, and the milk cow was making her way to the barn. The life of the ranch was steady and calm, the hours turning like pages in a book one has known and loved. And which one could return to, in need, all the days of a life.

"I will have to speak to my parents, of course. It is so sudden, and yet it's so exciting," Margaret answered finally, filled with elation and panic. One minute, expecting to wait out the winter on Cottonwood Ranch, riding the frost-rimed hills with her hands in her armpits for warmth, working on a needlework sampler or piecing a quilt from the bag of remnants and outgrown clothing; the next, anticipating a train ride across the breadth of America to meet new people and to learn a craft to take with her into the world.

Lying back on the ridge, Margaret looked into the sky. It had the look of a fall sky, the blue more subdued than summer's cerulean. High flights of geese skeined over daily now, and the hills rang with the sound of hunters' guns. Nicholas was watching her, leaning on one elbow, his hand sifting soil between his fingers. He was learning her face like his small vocabulary of her grandmother's words, one syllable at a time, by heart. Margaret stroked his face with her fingers, feeling the smooth slope of his jaw, the rough texture of his beard. He kissed her eyes, her cheek, and pulled a wisp of vetch from her hair. The ground still held the day's heat, though soon a hard frost would come in the night while the sunbrowned children slept and freeze the earth until spring. No more music of horned lark and meadowlark, no grace notes of blackbirds. The lovers held each other in the last hours of sunlight while the smell of crushed grass rose up around them, sweet and wild.

I have enough items now to begin planning their display. Some have been carefully washed, some backed with clean muslin, some placed in envelopes of Mylar, and others tentatively arranged on padded hangers. I have borrowed a sleigh bed and will make it up with the bed linens, draping a fragile nightdress, pleated and tucked, over the quilt which I've chosen to dress it. I have in the works a small catalogue with photographs, and our printer is working on display cards. The stories that arrived with some of the pieces will be printed as well so that both narratives, the written and the stitched, will interweave to create their own parable.

I've steadily made my way through Margaret's box and organized the material as much as I could. Sometimes I sit with my hands full of letters and cry for the girl whose shadow I see in every grove of ponderosa pines, whose hands I feel on my own hands as I smooth fabric and study photographs, a soft voice which I almost hear telling me of her difficulties in reading the light or how she wept herself when her first plate cracked. When I rode the high pastures, her arms circled my waist, helped me to find my old seat, to read the pressure needed to guide a horse on a flinty path. Was it her hair or my own that blew across my cheek as I let my horse gallop?

Chapter Eleven

A LETTER FROM THE ETHNOLOGY division of the Canadian Geological Survey, dated summer, 1907, asking if Miss Stuart would like to participate in field work among the Thompson, Okanagan and Shuswap tribes. Her photographic work has been recommended by Dr. Franz Boas in New York, and Dr. Edward Sapir has spoken highly of her data-collecting ability and mentions that her growing knowledge of the Thompson language will be of considerable value. The letter assures her that her fiancé will also be doing some work in the Spences Bridge area and can provide assistance if necessary.

The arrangements had been made. Margaret would travel to Spences Bridge with her father during the last week of November. From there she would take the train to Vancouver, then to Seattle, accompanied by relatives of Mr. Clemes in Spences Bridge who were returning home to San Francisco. Before leaving her, the relations would help her to board a transcontinental train that would take her to Chicago, then New York. Her concerns about the cost of such a trip had been dismissed by her father.

"When I inherited my father's money, there was some left over after I'd paid off the ranch and purchased more cattle and horses. I invested it on the advice of my banker in Kamloops, and it has done reasonably well. Money must not be a factor in your decision. And it must be *your* decision, finally, to make. There are not many opportunities in this valley for a young woman. Nursing, perhaps, if you were interested in that. The Royal Inland Hospital has recently begun to train nurses."

"No, Father, not nursing. I did think of teaching for a while, but I am really hopeful that I can do something useful with photography. Nicholas has said there will be a need for well-trained people to take accurate photographs for anthropology research. And perhaps I will even do commercial work, if I can find jobs. Miss Spencer has certainly made a name for herself in Kamloops and earns a good living doing something she loves."

William took his daughter's hand in his own and gave it an encouraging squeeze. "My dear, I think you will do exactly what you intend to. I am only sorry to see you leave us. Parents do not anticipate the going away of their children, and when the time comes, we feel bewildered. The house will not be the same, and I'll miss your company around the ranch."

"It won't be forever, Father. I'll be home in time to help take the cattle to the spring range, I'm sure."

What was unspoken between them was the possibility that she might not come back, or at least not as she had left — an unmarried girl, an older sister living among her family. Or that she would return altered by her experience of New York and its institutions of higher learning, its concert halls, museums and art galleries, into someone unknown to them, remote.

Nicholas returned to his home by train in mid-October, in time to travel through changing landscapes of shorn fields, trees losing their red and golden leaves to the air, expanses of tallgrass prairie white with frost near Fargo, North Dakota. He had written almost daily, long letters filled with news of his courses, lectures he'd attended, an exhibit he'd seen of the work of a group of photographers calling themselves the Photo-Secession Society, and he sent some copies of the magazine *Camera Work*, edited by Alfred Stieglitz and featuring the work of individual photographers — Stieglitz himself, Gertrude Kasebier, and Clarence H. White — so Margaret could share his pleasure. Margaret pored over the magazines, wondering how the effects in particular photographs had been achieved. She loved the orchard photographs of White and the portraits of Kasebier with their simple, evocative arrangements of children and women. One issue of *Camera Work* from earlier that year had sixteen photographs by a man called Steichen, portraits perfectly composed, each detail brilliant and singular. She loved the look of the magazine itself, its green cover with artistic lettering, and sometimes a reproduction on fine Japanese paper that you could remove and frame if you wished.

One letter spoke of an opera Nicholas had attended, *Dido and Aeneas*, by Henry Purcell. "My French grandmother loves this opera, and I was so pleased to be able to write to tell her I'd finally seen it. It was wonderful. There's a very moving final aria after Dido has said goodbye to Aeneas. She is about to die and sings,

> *When I am laid in earth,*
> *May my wrongs create*
> *No trouble in thy breast;*
> *Remember me, but ah!*
> *Forget my fate.*

I think everyone in the concert hall was weeping at that point, including me. Everything I see and hear speaks to me of you. I have written to your grandmother asking if she would make a basket for my father, one of the flat-backed ones that I always thought would make a good fishing creel. Will you bring it with you if she finishes it in time?"

Nicholas' mother had written a long friendly letter to the Stuarts. "We are so looking forward to having your daughter with us as long as it suits her heart. Please do not worry about her in our home. We already love her and will cherish her as her maman and papa do. We have been preparing a room, les petites sisters of Nicholas and I, making it pretty for the young lady to dream in. Our Nicholas is not the same young man who left us in the spring. He talks of horses and dried fish, telling us we would love both. Ah, la vie est belle when you are young, do you agree?"

The cattle drive went smoothly that year. After sorting, cutting out, and bringing the bred cows and yearling heifers down to overwinter at Culloden, the steers were taken to Kamloops over the Brigade Lake trail. Margaret rode the roan gelding and worked as hard as any of the hands. No stock wandered off to be given up as lost, none drowned, none ate the last blossoms of larkspur or milk vetch, and so they rode into Kamloops on the third morning with six hundred head of grass-fed steer to sell to the buyer, Pat Burns, who met them at the railyard corrals. Mr. Burns always sought out the Cottonwood beef for its consistent high quality and paid well — three and a half cents a pound that year for steers.

After the cowboys had loaded the cattle into the boxcars to be taken to Vancouver, they went to the nearest drinking establishment with the bonus William Stuart had paid them when he received his money. They would leave the next morning for the ranch, so they wanted to take advantage of their night on the town. Margaret and William had rooms at the Grand Pacific Hotel and planned to stay two nights in Kamloops, going back by stage with Angus Nelson after purchasing provisions for the ranch as well as the clothing Margaret needed to take with her to New York. She had made a list after talking to Mrs. Drake, a Nicola Lake resident who often spent her winters in Vancouver and who kindly gave her advice on what one wore in such surroundings and to the events Nicholas had mentioned they would attend — concerts, lectures, classes at the university. The first afternoon at the Grand Pacific, Margaret did nothing but bathe in the big tub, soaking off the dust of the trail, and then napped in the bed in the same room she had slept in the night of the Albani concert. (I know she listened to the creak of timbers beyond the dark ceilings as the building adjusted its weight, the peach-skin softness of the sheets on her shoulders . . .) So much had happened since then, too much to fathom as events remembered in clean singularity. Was she the same girl who had dressed in such excitement for the Opera House, who had spoken with the great singer, feeling shy as a meadowlark, and who had wondered what her future held as she rode the new mare along the sleeping streets of Kamloops at first light? The tree outside the window of her room, so shady and green in May, had shed its leaves but for a few which hung, withered and dry, in the autumn air.

While her father bought flour and supplies for mending harnesses, foot trimmers for the horses, and other items from a list he had prepared with Jenny, Margaret found the shop where she had bought trousers the previous May — John T. Beatton, Clothier — and bought dresses to supplement her rose muslin gown, one of dark blue and a simple green one of soft wool. The saleslady showed her some collars, one of lace, one of beaded silk, that could be worn with the green dress to make it versatile. Margaret also chose a grey wool skirt and jacket with black frogging and bought several yards of fine lawn to make into underclothes. The saleslady directed her to a cobbler, who fitted her with a pair of pretty black boots.

Her shopping completed, Margaret was free to spend an afternoon exploring the streets of Kamloops, which still held their allure. She wandered from street to street, looking at all the window displays, particularly the photographs in the window of Mary Spencer's photographic studio. She would have entered, asked questions, examined each piece of equipment she could see on the shelves inside, but the shop was closed, a sign requesting those interested in make appointments to telephone the proprietress at the given number. Margaret had never used a telephone and didn't feel courageous enough to ask at the hotel or post office how such a call might be made, so she contented herself with studying the photographs in the window as though they might tell her something of their origins. Wedding groups, portraits, a ceremony involving police officers, a shot of last year's May Queen and her handmaidens in their fancy white dresses: she looked at each shot, hoping to decode the image's individual elements, its composition and texture, the quality of light.

Meeting her father at dinner at the Grand Pacific, Margaret felt a pang of love for him, of gratitude that he was allowing her to try something new, undreamed of, unexperienced, of anticipated loneliness for his company during the next months. As if he knew what she was thinking, he patted her shoulder and gave her a kiss on the cheek.

"I remember the morning I left Astoria. It was raining, of course. It *always* rained in Astoria. My parents were still sleeping, and I crept past their bedroom and downstairs, leaving a letter for them on the dining table which was already laid for breakfast. I propped the letter against my father's coffee cup. It was white porcelain, I won't forget it, ever — the look of the letter against the cup, like something out of a novel, not a life. So I understand completely the desire you have to make something of yourself that is yours alone, not ours. Selfishly, however, I know how much I will miss you. You have been the best daughter a man could have, and never once did I regret that my first-born was not a son. You mean everything to us, and that is why we want you to go the way that you must."

"Did you regret the way you'd left, Father?"

William answered without hesitation. "I have no regrets about what I have done with my life, and I don't like to think of the man I'd have become had I not left my father's house. But the blessing of my family would have made my leaving less lonely, and that is why we give you ours."

Tears filled Margaret's eyes, and she hastily wiped at them with her table napkin. "Remember the day we bought Thistle? We sat at this very table for breakfast, and you asked if I'd go with you to look at her. I wonder what her foal will be. I hope she throws a filly. You must write to me immediately and tell me, and promise you'll allow me to name it."

"Agreed. And now I'm going to order champagne to toast my daughter's future."

Letters, a narrative of letters, dated and telling a breathless story of landscapes and buildings, bitter cold, a single light burning in a farm house somewhere on the great plain of America. A welcoming brick house filled with flowers and light, its tiny garden a testament to joy (roses tucked in against winter, an apple tree with the remnants of a nest cradled in its high branches, a wooden bench, a sundial of bronze incised *Grow old along with me, the best is yet to be* . . .), descriptions of concerts, a visit to the Little Gallery on Fifth Avenue, classes at Columbia and workshops in photographic technique, the taking of anthro-pomorphic measurements, linguistics, the shy declaration of an engagement and the description of a ring, the announcement of a return to begin a photographic assignment. *If this succeeds, and I am so hopeful that it might, I think we would like to live in the valley and work from there. With the telegraph and telephones becoming more common, it would be possible to keep in touch with the university and the American Museum of Natural History, for which Nicholas is doing some work.* Give unto them beauty for ashes, the oil of joy for mourning, the garment of praise for the spirit of heaviness. I feel heavy with the sorrow of what is to come, though my lungs have taken in fine seeds with the dry air and I have slept in a tent dusted with pollen, my body heavy with its golden profligacy.

At Spahomin, Margaret and her grandmother were preparing for a sweat bath. They had spread boughs of fir on the floor of the sweat lodge with some sage mixed in, and juniper from a special place known only to Grandmother Jackson. Placing the hot stones in the pit in the middle of the floor, they squatted to put their attention to cleansing their bodies and minds. Margaret felt her lungs sear as the hot dry air entered her chest, and she felt light headed in the intense heat. Her grandmother chanted a prayer in the Thompson language, asking that Margaret go with protection on her journey, that her own guardian spirit watch out for the girl, and her grandfather's, and all her ancestors at rest in the soil of the valley. A prayer had been said by Reverend Murray at Saint Andrew's Church the previous Sunday, asking that the Lord keep Margaret safe during her time away from them, and after the service people she had known all her life came to wish her Godspeed. After their sweat bath, the old woman and the young one washed with cold water and dried themselves with rough towels fashioned from sugar sacks. Riding home, Margaret felt clean and strong and curiously peaceful for the first time since she had made her decision to go to New York. She had been excited about the prospect from the first, but never with this deep knowledge that what she was doing was a necessary part of her progress into the next chapter of her life.

The morning Margaret and her father set out was clear and cold. August came to drive them to Nicola Lake, where they would take the stage to Forksdale and then to Spences Bridge. Jenny Stuart stood on the porch and embraced her daughter, then held her at arm's length to make sure she was ready to go. She stroked Margaret's face, the curve of cheek she had known and loved for seventeen years, and smoothed the wisps of black hair that framed the young face, committing to memory its detail and texture. Blind, she would know this daughter forever, her fingers alive with the instincts of birds. She kissed Margaret on each cheek and adjusted the collar of her travelling jacket. Margaret turned to her sisters.

"Goodbye, Mary, goodbye, Jane. You must help Mother in my place now. And Tom, you may ride Daisy while I'm gone, and take good care of her, please, and help Father. If Mother and Father write to tell me that you've been a help to them both, then I shall buy you something special in New York City and bring it home in my suitcase."

"A doll, Margaret, a doll, please?" Both sisters echoed the same wish.

"I don't know yet that you've been helpful. But I'm certain there will be dolls aplenty, just waiting to belong to girls who have helped their mother and not argued with each other."

And it was time to leave. Going along the lane that led out to the Douglas Lake road, Margaret tried to see everything at once — the barn, the chicken house, the cottonwoods with their remnants of magpie nests, the wide fields of Culloden dotted with the slumbering bodies of cattle among the bunch-grass and drowsy flies, horses watching the wagon as it commenced its journey, the family waving goodbye on the familiar porch, one of the ranch dogs running alongside, all of it knitted together by the wild clematis climbing up from the banks of the creek, fluffy seed heads blowing goodbye. If this was part of who she was, then what would she be without it? She had asked her grandmother the same question and was told that she must carry her home inside her. But she didn't know if she did, or could, never having left before in this way. In her suitcase, though, was her buckskin jacket and a little pouch she had made, decorated with quills given her by Alice and filled with dried sage, some strands of bunchgrass with the seeds intact, the drinking tube found at the gravesite, and a twist of paper with a spoonful of soil inside, gathered from the side of the creek. It would have to be enough.

They arrived at Spences Bridge late in the evening and went directly to Mr. Clemes's hotel, where rooms were waiting for them. They were introduced to the relations who would travel as far as Seattle with Margaret and spent some time drinking tea in the parlour, where a warm fire burned and a girl played the piano quietly while the talk went on about beef prices and progress. Mr. Clemes was an enthusiastic man, taking William out in the dark to admire again the red Woolsey he had arranged to have shipped from Paris after seeing it at the World Exposition in '98. Every visitor to the hotel was taken out to see the Woolsey, even if the visit was not the first. It was a fine automobile to drive around town, Mr. Clemes declared, as William examined the machine by lamplight and restrained his host from starting up the auto and taking it along the black streets with the same lamps held aloft.

In her bed that night, too excited to sleep, Margaret listened to the river. She had leaned out of the window earlier in the evening when she had been taken to the room with her luggage and had smelled the water, cold and flinty, as it raced towards its marriage with the Fraser at Lytton. Brown bats darted in under the eaves, feeding on the slow autumn flies and moths, almost ready to find a place to wait out the cold months. She thought of the big muscular fish in the Thompson's waters, swimming against the current, and the canoes guided by men darkened with charcoal and grease, going out to meet the fish at night with torches of pitch-pine. And on the talus slopes, even now the rattlesnakes were deep in their winter sleep under stones. How mysterious it was, the life of a place, with its rivers, trees and grasses, and the animals coming down to drink at dawn as they had done since time began. And just as mysterious, the sound of a train moving down the canyon, sounding its whistle as it passed through the town. People on that train, or one very similar to it, had witnessed a landslide, watched as innocent children were washed away by rising water. She wondered if they would see the site of the landslide as the train passed that way in the morning. And would she ever sleep?

She must have, because her father stood at her bedside with a cup of milky coffee, gently calling her to wake up. She drank the coffee gratefully, then dressed in the chilly morning air. Her stomach was a whole flock of butterflies fluttering their wings at once, some of them rising into her throat. Her hands shook as she buttoned her boots, and she forgot where she'd packed her hairbrush.

At the train station, the Clemes family stood to one side and chattered cheerfully amongst themselves, giving the Stuarts a private moment to say their goodbyes.

"You have everything? You're sure?"

"No, I'm not sure of anything, Father. But I think I have what I need. My cases, the camera, the ticket, money, yes, I think it's all here. But somehow I wish we were taking the stage together home to Nicola Lake. I feel nervous about this."

"I'm not surprised. This is a big venture for a girl who's more at home on a horse than anywhere. But everything will go well, I'm certain. You'll cable us from Seattle to say you've arrived? And from New York, of course?"

"Of course."

The train had arrived and the door of the carriage she would be boarding opened, the porter taking her baggage to stow it away. The Clemes relations stepped up to the carriage, waving to William and calling a final goodbye to Mr. Clemes. William embraced his daughter and helped her onto the platform stool and up the train steps. Margaret could say nothing but clung to her father's familiar arm until the last possible moment, when he pulled away, touched her shoulder, then hopped down to the platform. She waved a gloved hand and smiled through a mist that might have been tears or perhaps the beginning of rain glazing the window of the carriage. As the train pulled out of Spences Bridge, Margaret kept waving until her father was no longer visible. She sat where she could see the cluster of houses, hotels, the bridge itself, receding until the train rounded a corner and they were gone.

Are we remembered by mountains, the sweet fields of hay? Do we leave the syllables of our history in the lambent dawn or on the riffle of water as it moves past our feet in the shallows? A map of our lives might speak of favourite weather, the whistle of blackbirds on April mornings, the way our eyes saw colour, distinguished cloud forms, the texture of linen in a hoop of wood, stitched in and out by wildflowers. Our mark on the map might be rough trails or roads, open pastures, a wild cartography of longing. In Margaret's box, a street map of New York with tiny birds sketched in and a few trees on significant quadrangles as she provided her own icons for the city. Or our history might be followed as a series of threads, silk, wool, fine textiles or rags, which outline the shapes our lives have taken — the samplers of girlhood, the tea towels of domesticity, quilts of practical warmth, and the yoking together of joy and grief in the long recollection of age. *As for man, his days are as grass: as a flower of the field, so he flourisheth.*

Because she had asked him to, the porter pointed out the site of the landslide to Margaret as the train passed — a raw slash of debris on the side of the river. Under that debris, there were houses crushed like brittle cottonwood twigs, even a child flattened like a wildflower between the pages of a book. She pressed her face to the window, seeing the field of the dead passing quickly as the train gathered speed. The river moved in urgent currents, oblivious to all that happened, ungoverned by memory. Margaret could see the yellow blooms of rabbitbrush persisting in the cold days of November and a tangle of the wild clematis she loved, which some called traveller's joy, wrapped around a dead pine tree on the slope above the river.

Light began to enter the canyon as the sun rose high enough to illuminate the dark cliffs and narrow valleys of creeks leading into the Thompson from their sources in the dark mountains. At times, it felt as though the train was moving through a tunnel roofed by sky, so close were the walls of the mountains. The porter reeled off names as they passed creeks and town sites or entered tunnels in the shoulders of the rocks. Skoonka, Drynoch, Nicomen, Thompson Landing. Margaret was thrilled to hear the names, like lyrics to the music of the train. At Lytton she saw the azure waters of the Thompson enter the Fraser and lose themselves in the muddy confluence. At one time, her grandmother told her, so many campfires burned along the sides of these rivers that anyone looking down from a mountain must have thought the sight a fallen constellation, a wash of light along the dark water. She thought of George Edwards riding down to prison, manacled, passing the same rocks, the same trees, with an early summer sky overhead. The newspaper had said that everyone knew which train carried him to New Westminster, and bystanders called from each stopping place, wishing him well; even the dogs remembered him.

The Clemes relations talked animatedly in their seats, and they called to Margaret to come and share their snack. Little cakes and tarts filled a basket, along with thin cucumber sandwiches. Margaret wasn't hungry but accepted an apple, choosing a fine Wolf River with a deep red skin. The train was carrying a shipment of apples from the Clemes orchard, the Martel ranch, and Mrs. Smith's trees to customers in Vancouver. At Lytton, they'd stopped to pick up hundreds of boxes from Earlscourt Farm, and when the porter opened the door of their carriage, the smell of apples filled the air like balm. Hell's Gate, China Bar, Kanaka, Keefer, Slaughter Run, Alexandra Bridge. Biting into her apple, imagining she detected the flavour of sunlight and sage behind the crisp white flesh veined with rose, Margaret watched the passing hills, falling asleep just as the train left the canyon to begin the straight run through the Fraser Valley to Vancouver.

Epilogue

IN A HIGH PASTURE OVERLOOKING the canyon, horses graze, ankle deep in forage, while the fertile wind lifts their tails, enters them as surely as wind entered the fleetfooted mares of Lusitania. A solitary girl might be sitting on a slope above the river as the train passes, a fierce pulse running through her. Was it the pulse of the train or was the earth echoing, loud with the lives contained inside the body? Some were bound, knees to chin, with slender twine made from the fibrous roots of mountain spruce, some buried alive as infants in cradles of bark, soil entering their nostrils and ears, the small socket of their eyes. And girls taken early by influenza in a private enclosure of white pickets, overlooking the river of their birth, their lives contained in a parenthesis of wind: 1889-1908; wild rye shifting in the air; *the beautiful uncut hair of graves.* What secrets do the hills contain in their suede hollows, what mysteries are lifted from the stones in the unbearable stillness of morning? *Which is the way where light dwelleth? and as for darkness, where is the place thereof?* My daughter has rolled into the grassy hollow of the kikuli pit at Nicola Lake, closing her eyes as she imagines the life of its ghostly household in the time we nearly know as we sit on the shore of the lake. Looking up, she sees a fresh moon in the daylight sky, hears the girls singing wherever they might be — in memory, in photographs, crumbling bones under a cairn of boulders, a little necklace of elk teeth at what was once a youthful throat, in the heart, the imagination. *You remind me of a girl I once watched picking flowers.* On the shoulders of the young girls, golden pollen; in their hair, a halo of seeds, ruffled by the breeze. If we are very quiet, they might sing to us, dry husks in the wind, dust of stars.

ACKNOWLEDGEMENTS

I am indebted to my family and friends for boundless encouragement and willingness to listen, advise and go on trips in search of a road, a plant, weather. The British Columbia Arts Council provided financial support for which I am grateful. Staff at the Provincial Archives, the Kamloops Museum and the Nicola Valley Museum and Archives were very helpful in answering queries as well as tracking down maps and information. I was also lucky to have Laurel Boone for an editor. Her enthusiasm and careful eye helped me to make this a better book.